Bob Moseley

OUT OF BOUNDS

outskirtspress
DENVER, COLORADO

This book is dedicated to my beautiful wife Sheila for her steadfast support and encouragement to see this writing project through.

I would also like to thank Ken Dixon, a journalistic pro if there ever was one, for his feedback on the story, plus writers group members Brian Blake, Sari Bodi and Tracy Porosoff for their valuable input.

A sincere thank you goes out to Shelton (Conn.) High School teacher Carolyn Finley for graciously allowing me to observe her journalism class and the production of the award-winning student newspaper Gael Winds. Also, Lt. Robert Kozlowsky of the Shelton Police Department for helping me to authenticate certain scenes.

I sat alone in the baseball dugout, my ears searching for a voice—no matter how distant—my eyes straining for a silhouette to emerge on the horizon. "Deep Throat," my mysterious source for the entire four-month investigation, was about to be revealed on a blustery, gray March afternoon.

I checked the time on my cell phone. The note said to meet at 4 p.m., and it was now 4:05. *Don't blow me off!*

The snow on the pitcher's mound had nearly melted away, leaving a muddy mess. My story was a muddy mess, too, unless I could confirm my explosive information. I had to meet my Deep Throat face to face.

This wasn't some puffy high school feature I was writing. It was hard news! It could result in jail time, for God's sake!

Where is he—or she?

Suddenly I heard footsteps ... and a shadow crept forward from behind the dugout.

—◆—

CHAPTER 1

When I first heard the names Woodward and Bernstein, they sounded like some kind of law firm to me. I had no idea who Bob Woodward and Carl Bernstein were. I still can't believe they changed my life forever, sparking my greatest triumph—and also a period of soul-searching pain.

I was sitting in Mr. McCloud's journalism class at Hillsboro High, and my knee was starting to act up. The surgery to repair my anterior cruciate ligament—better know as the ACL—was just months old and I was limping around like a wounded duck. But at least I wasn't on crutches anymore. I adjusted my knee brace and stretched out as the movie was about to begin.

" 'All the President's Men' stars Robert Redford and Dustin Hoffman as the *Washington Post* reporters, Woodward and Bernstein," Mr. McCloud told the class, as he popped in the DVD and hit the lights. "This film was nominated for Best Picture in 1976, and it gives a sharp portrayal of actual events, possibly the most important reporting in American history."

"Why was it so important?" the girl next to me asked.

"You'll see," McCloud replied. "What started out as a probe into a minor break-in at the Democratic Party national headquarters led to investigative reporting that resulted in the resignation of the 37th president of the United States, Richard Nixon, in 1974. The reporters exposed corruption that became known as the Watergate scandal."

Watergate? It sounded like some kind of a dam that burst. And after seeing the movie, and discussing it in class, I realized it had. A dam burst exposing political corruption, forever changing the way Americans view government, and a dam burst on my future. I was flooded with dreams.

I, Jason Jefferson, had to be an investigative reporter.

I stuck around after the bell, to talk to Mr. McCloud. "Those guys were so cool, exposing corruption like that," I said. "They did something *really* important."

"Yeah, they were extraordinary reporters, Jason," he replied. "The funny thing is it started out looking like a routine burglary, but Woodward had the instincts to dig deeper. The more he found out, the bigger the story became. They exposed a conspiracy cover-up ordered by President Nixon."

"And it wasn't just Nixon involved," I pointed out. "It looked like the whole government was behind it."

"What's really shocking is the FBI and the Department of Justice seemed to go along with it. And a former attorney general—the chief law enforcement officer in the country— was directly involved in breaking the law. John Mitchell went to jail."

"How about that source who kept giving Woodward information anonymously, the 'Deep Throat' character," I pointed out.

"Yes, that was all true. The identity of 'Deep Throat' was finally revealed in 2005, about 30 years later. We'll talk about that tomorrow in class."

"Cool! At first I thought the movie was too old. I mean, they didn't even have computers or cell phones back then."

"Right, you saw they used typewriters."

"But I loved the suspense. Woodward and Bernstein were like maniacs going after that story," I added. "They never backed down."

"That's the mark of good reporters," McCloud said. "You have to be persistent —even relentless — and inquisitive. Plus, you have to make hard choices. They knew their investigation could bring down a whole presidency, ruining lives. They were in danger as well."

"Could someone have killed them, trying to keep the story from coming out?" I asked.

"You never know," McCloud said. "At the very least, journalists run the risk of making enemies when they honestly report stories."

It all sounded so exciting, the snooping around to uncover the truth. But then my fantasy was shattered by a reality check. The bell rang for Period 4.

"You better get to your next class," McCloud reminded me. He obviously had an off period himself.

"Oh ... yeah. I'm gonna be late. Could you write me a pass, please?"

"I don't usually do this, Jason, but here you go," he said, scribbling his initials on a blue pad of paper and pushing it my way. "I'm glad you enjoyed the movie so much."

As I headed toward the door with my pass, hurrying off to Spanish, I heard McCloud call my name.

"Hey, Jason. If you really like journalism, you should join the school newspaper. We have a lot of fun."

And that's how it all began.

CHAPTER 2

It was fall, and I missed football badly. For the first time in my life, I wasn't playing. All because I blew out my knee in May. It wasn't even a contact drill. It was the week of spring practice; we weren't wearing pads. I made a sharp cut on our artificial turf while running with the ball. My cleat must have caught a seam or something, because I heard something pop and my knee just gave out. Doctors later told me it was a torn ACL.

Greg Maxwell was the first one to help me.

"Hang on Jason. Don't put any pressure on it," he said as he carried me, all 160 pounds, off the field like a wounded soldier.

Greg was 6-foot-1 and 215 pounds of pure muscle. I'll never forget how easily he scooped me up all by himself, taking care to prop up the knee. I wasn't in horrible pain at the time, but I knew something wasn't right.

The doctor said forget about football for at least a year. He might as well have said, "Find a new life." After I scored 10 touchdowns as a halfback on the freshman team the previous fall, Coach Dawson said he couldn't wait to get me on varsity. His exact words were I was so quick I could "walk into

a room, hit the light switch, and be in bed before it got dark."
I was *so* stoked about being with the varsity as a sophomore.

Who wouldn't be? Winning isn't a goal at Hillsboro
High, it's a tradition. And I wanted desperately to be a part
of that tradition. Over the past 20 years, Hillsboro had won
more state football championships than any school in Illinois. With guys like Greg returning, next year's team was
going to be awesome.

Greg was heading into his junior year, but he was already
a stud. Coach Dawson raved about his potential, saying he
was one hellacious linebacker with unlimited potential.
Some of the guys on the team even called him "The Barbarian" because of his long hair and the way he ruthlessly
sacked quarterbacks.

To me, Greg was always the guy from my neighborhood
who I looked up to, kind of like a big brother, I guess. I could
turn to him for advice. One time, when he saw me hanging
around Justin Walker, he told me to stay away from him,
that the kid was trouble. He was right; Walker got arrested
at 17 for trying to rob a convenience store.

Greg used to come over to the house and recruit me for
tackle games on the field at the corner of Brighton and Travers. Greg was a grade older, and a lot bigger, but I'd join him
and the older kids, even though I knew I'd take a pounding.
I didn't want to look like I was scared, and I wanted to be
part of the gang. Who knows, maybe I developed my speed
that way—running for my life trying to escape tacklers.

I'd come home covered with grass stains and my hoodie stretched out or ripped from guys grabbing to bring me down. My mom made me wear an old one.

Greg was everything I wanted to be — a star football player. The only difference was he played defense and I played offense.

——◆——

I was crushed with football out of the picture. I desperately needed something to fill the void. That's where Mr. McCloud's journalism class came in. I figured if I couldn't play I could at least write about sports. I took McCloud up on his offer and checked out the school newspaper after school.

"Welcome, Jason!" McCloud said, getting up from his desk to greet me as I poked my head into his classroom. Located in the basement of the school, McCloud's windowless classroom was always a beehive of activity, hosting journalism and English classes and serving as the *Hillsboro Herald* newsroom.

"I'll introduce you to Gina Giantoli," he said. "She's right over here."

I looked to where he pointed, but all I saw was the back of a head.

"Gina, do you know Jason? He's interested in joining our staff as a reporter," McCloud, the newspaper advisor, said as he walked me over to a bank of a dozen Mac computers rimming the far wall.

"Sure, Mr. McCloud," Giantoli replied, looking up from her computer. A brief smile sprung from her angular, businesslike face.

"Gina's our editor-in-chief at the *Herald*. She does a superb job; I trust her completely," McCloud said, turning toward me. "She'll get you started."

Then McCloud was gone. "Meghan, you need to move the placement of this ad," he called out, striding across the room. Gina looked back down at her computer screen.

"I'll be with you in a minute," she said, frowning. "I've got to finish editing this story. I'm on deadline."

While she typed I looked up at an enlarged quote written in script across the wall: "I may disapprove of what you say, but I will defend to the death your right to say it." — Voltaire.

Of the 10 or so people in the room, some were designing pages, while others wrote stories, checked paper layouts mounted on a countertop, or edited. A couple of kids looked like they were goofing off on YouTube, but everybody else seemed busy.

"Okay, Jefferson, I'm free," Gina finally said after making me wait a good five minutes. "So you want to write?"

"Yeah. Do you have any stories you want covered?"

"I've got one that we could start you out with," she said.

"Great! What is it?"

"I hear the cafeteria is considering a menu change from French fries to tater tots. Maybe you can check it out?"

I stood there with my mouth open. "You're kidding me, right?"

"Not at all. Tater tots may not be sexy, but it's news that affects everybody at Hillsboro. Maybe there are other changes in the food too."

"But I want to do investigative stories," I protested.

"This is investigative! You're investigating the cafeteria," Gina shot back.

"Yeah, maybe I'll find they're putting cyanide in the sloppy Joes," I said, as sarcastically as possible.

"Look, if you don't want to do it then just forget it. I know you want to be Woodward and Bernstein — I saw the movie, too, you know — but you're only a sophomore. You're a cub; you start at the bottom. Maybe when you're a senior you can investigate Principal Healey and break the news that he's embezzling school funds. Hah!"

"Don't you have anything else?"

"That's your story, take it or leave it."

"All right, all right, I'll do it." It was a lame assignment, but at least I'd get my first byline.

The next day, I ambled down to the cafeteria during my free seventh period to interview the head of food services. It seemed strange to see the place so quiet and deserted. The cafeteria staff was gone by then, and the lady in charge ushered me into her cramped office. I sidestepped food containers and boxes that rose to the ceiling. On her desk were stacks of order forms.

"So, what is it you'd like to know?"

"Are you taking French fries off the menu and replacing them with tater tots?" I asked. The sound of the question made me cringe. How stupid!

"As a matter of fact we are," she replied.

"Why's that?" I asked half-heartedly.

"We can realize some cost savings, and tater tots aren't as greasy, so they're healthier," the lady said. "But that's just one of the changes around here."

For the next 30 minutes, I was scribbling notes down, filling five pages of my notebook. I felt a little better when I left.

A few days later, after I turned the story in, Gina got back to me with some feedback.

"Do you know you spelled the lady's name wrong? It's Jenkens with an 'e' not an 'i.' You spelled it J-e-n-k-i-n-s."

"Sorry," I offered.

"That's inexcusable, not getting the name right. And you also had some grammatical errors. Don't you know the difference between there, their and they're by now?"

"Of course, I do. I must not have proofread it," I said defensively. "I didn't have time. You told me the deadline was Wednesday."

"Always give it a second read," she scolded. "Also, you inserted your opinion in a hard news story. I took out the part where you wrote, 'Getting rid of French fries is a real mistake.' "

"All right, but aside from that how was the story?" I didn't expect lavish praise, but I thought I did do a pretty good job of turning the lemon she handed me into lemonade.

"It was all right for a first assignment," she grudgingly conceded, her voice lightening. "You uncovered a few things."

The next week, after my story was out in print, Julie Briscoe, another reporter on the *Herald* staff, came up to me.

"I really liked your story on the food service," she said, offering a warm smile.

"You did?"

"Yeah, it was great. That's so cool that they're bringing in a salad bar. The girls will love it."

"Maybe the girls will, but I don't think you'll see guys racing to it," I said.

"Are they really going to get rid of the soda machines?"

"They're threatening to. They're on some health kick to fight obesity."

"No w-a-a-a-y. That would suck. I'm addicted to diet soda."

"Tell me about it. But nothing's final yet. The school may decide it loves the money from Pepsi and Coke more."

Julie, a tall girl with a fashion sense borrowed from the hippie era, pulled back her long brown hair, which flowed halfway down her back. She wore little to no makeup. "Anyway, your story had a lot of useful information," she said. "I really liked it!"

"Thanks. I'm happy to hear someone say that. Gina kind of trashed it."

"She did? Don't worry about it," Julie said, waving her hand dismissively. "Gina is kind of cranky sometimes. She's a senior and she thinks she's hot stuff."

"She's giving me crappy assignments. Now she wants me to do a puff piece on the new Prayer Club," I pointed out. "I really want to do investigative reporting. I want to uncover some dirt."

"Well, keep up the good reporting. Maybe you will," Julie said, smiling as she waved goodbye.

As she flitted away, a crazy thought entered my mind: I wondered if Woodward and Bernstein started out reporting on tater tots?

CHAPTER 3

How in the world was I going to get 1,000 words on the Prayer Club? There wasn't that much to write about. All they did was get together before school and pray.

I met with a girl named Lisa Halloran, who was head of the Prayer Club—the Pope, I liked to call her.

"I'm so glad to meet y-o-o-o-u," she said with a smile. "God bless you for interviewing me."

"Uh ... thanks," I replied, not knowing how to respond to a "God bless you," unless it was after a sneeze. "My editor assigned me to do it."

"Well, I'm glad they did! Maybe when people see the story, we'll get some new members!"

"Why did you form the Prayer Club?" I asked, whipping out the obvious first question. It wasn't exactly penetrating, but it warmed things up.

"They don't allow prayer in classes, but we believe it's our constitutional right to be able to assemble and pray," Lisa said. "There are only six of us, and we're very committed."

"Is it just Christians?"

"Right now it is, but we welcome all religions," she replied.

"What kind of things do you pray about?"

"Oh, it's up to the individual. But as a group we usually pray for peace and the health of family and friends."

"Anybody ever pray they'll pass calculus?" I couldn't resist that one.

"Not that I know of," Lisa said with a laugh, "but they can if they want to."

"Do you think the school should change the rules and have prayer in class?" I asked, baiting my hook. I was hoping she would say 'yes' and stir up some controversy — give me something to write about.

"Not necessarily. I understand the separation of church and state," Lisa answered.

She wasn't biting, and before long I was running out of questions. The interview was going nowhere. How was I even going to put together a story?

I stared at Lisa, who was dressed conservatively in a white blouse, dark blue sweater and skirt down to her knees. She wore black secretarial-type glasses, and looked out-of-step with the rest of the student body. She seemed very nice, but I began to wonder if she'd ever been out on a date.

My list of prepared questions was soon depleted. Finally, out of desperation, I threw out, "Does your club ever get any flak from the other students?" I expected a quick "no." Why would anyone care?

But Lisa surprised me. "We do. We get harassed by some kids who don't understand us."

"Really?" I straightened up in my chair and leaned forward. "What do they do?"

"We've been called Bible-thumpers, Jesus Freaks, and Prayer Geeks. One time someone shouted at us when we met in the courtyard, "Pray that you'll get a life!"

"That's awful," I said.

"It is. Something happens almost every time we meet," Lisa revealed. "But what did Jesus say? Forgive them, for they know not what they do."

She went on to tell me about other incidents of harassment, and I began to sympathize with her. These kids weren't hurting anyone. Why were they being picked on?

"Sometimes we even pray that God forgives the ignorant," Lisa said.

I suddenly had an angle for my story. Churning out 1,000 words was going to be no problem. In fact, I wished I had more space.

In the next edition of the *Herald* the headline read: Prayer Club faces harassment.

"That's some story. I've heard kids talking about it," Julie said, pulling me over in the hallway between classes.

"Thanks, Julie. Yeah, the Pope gave me some good quotes."

"You mean Lisa?"

"Yeah."

"Well, I don't blame her for telling somebody. It sucks how they get picked on."

"I hear ya. People should respect them more."

Julie was rapidly becoming my closest friend on the newspaper. She was a sympathetic sounding board for my gripes about Gina and the assignments I got. A sophomore like me, Julie didn't get great stories, either, so we were in the same boat, rowing against a tide of seniority.

"Gina *has* to like this story. She can't treat you like a cub reporter anymore, not after this and the cafeteria story."

After school, a couple of days later, Gina called me over in the "newsroom." I was about to find out.

"Well, you created quite a stir with that story on the Prayer Club, Jason," she said, looking me in the eye for a change. However, her expression didn't exactly convey gratitude.

"Yeah, kids are really talking about it," I remarked. "That's what we want, isn't it?"

"Just as long as it doesn't lead to more harassment. Then you made it worse."

"I don't think it will. Kids are sympathetic to them now."

"Maybe, but you inserted your opinion again, and that's not your job. That's what we have editorial writers for. I had to cut out the part where you said students should be ashamed of themselves. They don't need you to tell them that, Jefferson."

"Sorry," I said, but I didn't mean it. A reporter has to have some freedom to say what he thinks.

"Well, you took a nice angle, and like I said, you got kids talking," Gina conceded. "We've even had some hits on our website."

"Thanks!" I was a little bowled over by Gina's ounce of praise. Maybe it wasn't a rave review, but coming from her it was something.

"You showed good reporter's instincts and raised an important issue. I'm writing a column for our next paper condemning the Prayer Club harassment."

It figures, I thought. Gina's jumping in to hijack my story. She'll probably use my opinions too.

But I now had some clout. It was time to use it. "Gina, can I try writing a sports feature?" I asked.

"You're tired of news already?" she responded, looking like her old annoyed self again.

"No, it's not that. You know I'd love to do a good, long investigative story on something. But until that comes around it might be fun to do something on the football team. They're really kicking butt."

"I know. But Steven Choi is the sports editor. He handles that section. Go talk to him."

I really didn't know Steven at all, but he was willing to listen.

"I was a football player, too, before I tore my ACL, and I'm hoping to play again next year after it heals," I pointed out.

"Tough break, dude," he said. "But I guess if you can't play you can always write about it."

I nodded in agreement.

"I'll tell you what, we've been meaning to do a feature on Pete Cruz, the linebacker. He's having an awesome year. Why don't you do something on him?"

"Yeah, he's good, but what about Greg Maxwell, the other linebacker? He's playing great too," I immediately pointed out.

"The Barbarian? You're right, he is. But I want to hold off on Maxwell. He's just a junior and Cruz is a senior. Go with the veteran, man."

"Okay." I was just happy to be writing sports for a change.

I passed Pete Cruz in the hall the next day and set something up. "How 'bout after practice on Wednesday?" I suggested.

"Yeah, you can catch me when we come off the field," he said.

First, I wanted to talk to Coach Dawson and get some quotes, so I grabbed him before practice that day.

He greeted me warmly. "Hey there, Jason. How's that knee recovering?"

"Good, Coach. I plan on playing again next year."

"Good for you! That's the right attitude, son. You gotta stay positive, and stick with the rehab."

Coach Dawson invited me into his office and we sat down. "Now, you wanted to ask me about Pete Cruz for the *Herald*?

Coach Dawson proceeded to pile on the praise. "Pete's a big reason why we're 5-0. Our defense has only allowed one touchdown," he pointed out. "Outstanding!"

"I know. I've been to every game," I said, not wanting to look like I'd abandoned the program after my injury.

"Look at this," he said, pushing a piece of paper in front of me. "I got this today — a letter from Oklahoma State asking me about Petey. And a few days ago we got one from the University of Maryland. Colleges are all interested in him."

"Do you think he can play Division I football?" I asked.

"He's got the talent and desire, he just needs to get bigger and stronger. I think Petey goes about six-feet, 205 pounds now, but he may still grow. Those schools must think he will, or else they think he can play another position besides linebacker. He's a pretty fair fullback, too."

"Yeah I know. He's tough to bring down," I acknowledged.

I veered off course. The interview was about Pete Cruz, but I couldn't help but ask Coach Dawson about my friend Greg. "What about Greg Maxwell? Are colleges interested in him too?"

"You bet. Even though he's only a junior, schools are hot on his trail. In fact, I get more mail asking about Greg than Petey."

"Wow. What schools are after Greg?"

"I got a call from Notre Dame the other day," the coach said. "Not too shabby."

"Notre Dame!" I gasped. I imagined the sight of Greg in a gold helmet, charging out of the tunnel before 80,000 screaming fans in Notre Dame Stadium, the Irish fight song playing. That would be his dream come true.

I resisted my urge to ask more questions about Greg. After all, the interview *was* supposed to be about Pete. Five minutes later, I had plenty of quotes from Coach Dawson, and I could tell he was eager to head out to practice.

"I hope we'll see you back at spring practice, Jason," he said as we left his office. "You can come back from an ACL. Don't get down."

"I won't, coach." His encouragement stroked my ego. He acted like he wanted me back on the team.

I figured I'd watch all of practice, so I sat down on the bleachers, soaking in the color of a gorgeous late September day. I started to review my notes, but it wasn't long before I had a visitor.

"Hi, Jason," came a voice from below. I lifted my head. There was Sara Cooley, Greg's girlfriend. She looked cute, as always, wearing a yellow shirt, open brown vest and tight jeans. Her brown eyes sparkled like she was really happy to see me. A light breeze tossed her short, stylish auburn hair.

"Hey, Sara. What's up?"

"Nothing much. Just watching practice. Awesome day!"

Sara chatted me up about school and my knee. She was always very sweet — and crazy about Greg. I think they first hooked up in eighth grade. That's like dating for a century by high school standards.

"Coach Dawson told me Notre Dame is recruiting Greg," I remarked.

"They sure are! He's getting letters from all over the country, even calls sometimes," Sara said. "Greg can't keep up with it all."

"It must be so cool ... to be wanted by everyone."

Sara paused for a minute. I could tell she was considering something important. "It's kind of scary, in a way," she confessed. "I want to go where he goes, and who knows where that will be? We've always talked about going to college together, but now he's getting so much attention ... I don't want to ever lose Greg."

I tried to reassure her. "You won't."

Sara smiled back at me, as if to say thanks.

A while later, I got up and said goodbye. I wanted to get down to the field early to make sure I caught Pete as he came off practice. Only problem was, I accidentally kicked one of Sara's books as I dragged my bad leg. The book — "Introduction to Physics," ironically — plummeted between the rows of bleacher seats and through the maze of girders below.

"Oh, my bad, Sara. I'll get it," I said.

But she wouldn't hear of it. "No, go get ready for your interview. I can get it. No problem."

Coach Dawson blew his whistle a few minutes before 5:30 p.m. "Okay, line up for wind sprints," he ordered. Half a dozen whistles later, players started jogging off the field, pulling off their helmets and sucking wind. Some rushed for the locker room, while others moved at a turtle's pace.

"Hey, Jason! What's up man?"

"Nothing much, Greg. I'm here interviewing for a story."

"On what?"

"They want me to do something on Pete Cruz for the *Herald*. I gotta get him after practice."

"How's the knee?"

"Getting better."

"Well, good luck man. I wanna see a full recovery." With that Greg turned his attention to Sara, who was approaching from our left. She rushed up and kissed him, even though Greg was a sweaty, smelly mess.

"Pete, got a minute?" Cruz was already past me, heading for the locker room when I caught his attention.

"Oh yeah, Jefferson. Where do you want to do this?" I motioned him over to the bleachers, where we sat down.

"Don't forget to mention me in the story," Curtis Jones, a senior wide receiver, joked when he saw what we were doing. At least I think he was joking.

As we began to talk, it became clear that Pete Cruz was no shrinking violet. But what linebacker would be?

"I feel I'm the best in the conference, and the best player in the state," Cruz bragged. "There are a lot of colleges after me."

"I know. I talked to Coach Dawson," I noted.

"An assistant coach from Maryland is coming over to our house next week, but I'm not sure I want to go there. I think I can do better."

I jotted down his quotes on my notepad, and Pete seemed totally unconcerned. He rambled on, talking looser than a girl at a slumber party.

"We're the best team in the state, no doubt about it," he crowed. "I even think we deserve votes for a national ranking in the *USA Today* poll."

As I furiously scribbled down his quotes, I felt a surge inside. This was great copy! I could envision some of these lines as callouts, the enlarged quotes we sometimes run.

"There are a lot of underclassmen on the team, too. Do you think Hillsboro could be even better next year?" I asked.

Pete looked at me with a smirk that seemed to say, how can the team be better without me?

"I mean ... uh, Greg Maxwell's coming back, so the linebacking corps should be real strong again." I didn't dare bring up that Coach Dawson thought Greg could potentially be better than Pete.

Cruz looked at me funny again. Then a putdown rushed out of his mouth.

"I'm the middle linebacker. Maxwell plays outside. A lot of times he makes the tackle because I'm double-teamed."

I looked up from my notes and stared him in the eyes. "So you think Greg is overrated?"

"Yeah," he shot back. "I'm not saying he's not good, but I take on all the blockers. He just runs to the ball. Sometimes he's not even blocked. When he blitzed for that second sack on Saturday, nobody even touched him."

Whoa! Somebody was green with jealousy.

"I think the scouts and anybody who knows football can see who's really the best linebacker out there."

"And college? Are you confident you can play at a big school?" I asked.

"Sure am. I just need to gain more weight and strength to go big-time, but I will. You can count on it."

By now the field had emptied and we were the only people in the bleachers. The sun was headed down. We talked a little more, but I had my story. And it looked hot, like Page One material.

"You got everything?" asked Pete. "I gotta go before they close the locker room."

"Yeah, thanks for your time," I replied. Cruz just grunted, grabbed his helmet and rushed off.

I limped behind him, but at the same time, I felt a new spring in my step.

CHAPTER 4

"Jason, wait!"

I looked back over my shoulder as I headed down to journalism class. Lisa Halloran was winding her way through the hallway, slipping through gaps between students like a halfback picking a hole.

"Sorry!" she said, after knocking into a guy. "Are you all right?" Like a bump from little Lisa was really going to hurt him.

"Jason, I just wanted to thank you for the article on the Prayer Club. We've gotten great feedback."

"You have?"

"Absolutely. Some people have asked me about joining, and best of all, it seems like the harassment has stopped. The power of the pen ..."

She smiled so sweetly, I felt a warm feeling inside. "I'm glad I could help you," I said.

"Well, God bless you. I don't want to make you late for class."

That was an unexpected offering of gratitude, and it surprised me that I really had made a difference. But the Prayer

Club was small potatoes; my piece on Pete Cruz was going to really make waves. Students at Hillsboro High would all know the name Jason Jefferson after that got printed. I was sure they would look for my byline.

I approached journalism class just as the bell sounded. Julie Briscoe, my fellow cub reporter, got to the door at the same exact time. "You first, Sir Limp-A-Lot," she said, motioning with her hand.

Mr. McCloud looked up and smiled as we entered the room. I plopped down in the front row seat I grabbed on the first day of school, back when I was on crutches.

"I want you to take a look at the quote on the board, think about it and tell me what you think it means," McCloud told the class.

The inscription read: "I have made this letter longer than usual, only because I have not had the time to make it shorter."

"It doesn't make sense," someone said.

"Oh, yes it does. Think about it," McCloud responded.

"Does it mean that longer isn't always better?" I guessed.

"In a way, Jason," McCloud said. "This quote comes from a French philosopher named Blaise Pascal who lived in the 17th century. In some ways it embodies the essence of journalism."

"It's about editing!" I called out in a confident voice.

"Yes it is," McCloud said, nodding his head to me. "In journalism, as in a well-written letter, we strive for brevity, or an economy of words. We want to eliminate any extraneous words. Often, by making something shorter, you make it read better. It becomes crisp, vibrant copy."

He talked some more about editing, and we proceeded to work on an editing exercise until class was almost over. Then McCloud delivered an announcement.

"I've arranged for a guest speaker on Friday. Miles Cannon from News Channel 4 will be speaking to our class."

The announcement created a buzz in class. "Wow! I watch him all the time," one girl said. Not me. I hardly knew who he was. I didn't watch network news, but I knew the ESPN broadcasters by heart.

"Try to come up with at least one good question for Mr. Cannon in advance," McCloud said. "You can ask him just about anything to do with journalism, except his salary."

"Why not that? I bet he makes big bucks," Angelo Scotto blurted out.

"Because that's pri-i-i-i-vate," McCloud answered, drawing out the last word for emphasis. "Would you want someone knowing how much you make?"

"I don't care. It's $7.95 an hour at Burger King. Just call me Bill Gates," Scotto joked, puffing out his chest.

The bell rang, and before I could even collect my stuff, Gina came storming into the room for Journalism II class. She was in so fast, it almost seemed like she was perched outside, waiting to pounce.

"Gina, I'm almost done with my story on Cruz. You'll get it soon," I said.

"It doesn't go to me. It's a sports story. It goes to Steven," she said, abruptly turning away.

"I think this guy Cannon is pretty lame. He's just a talking head," Julie said as we headed out.

"I wouldn't know. I've never seen him," I replied.

"So, what are you working on now?"

"I've got a sports feature coming up that's going to be BIG," I assured her. "If the Prayer Club story caused a stir, this one will be an earthquake."

"Cool! I'll be looking for it. See you later, Jason."

That feature felt like a winning Lotto ticket in my hands. I couldn't wait to turn it in.

I stayed after school and finished writing my story on the computer in journalism class. Mr. McCloud was hanging around grading papers, but we were the only ones in the room.

"Got hot copy there Jason?" he inquired.

"I sure do. It's a sports story this time."

"Really? What's it on?"

"It's a feature on the football team. I got some great quotes." I didn't want to reveal too much. McCloud could always squash stories if he thought they were too controversial.

"Well, just make sure they're accurate. You don't want to put words in somebody's mouth. That's libel."

"Oh, they're accurate," I said, never raising my head from the computer screen.

"That's all you need. Did you tape-record the interview?" McCloud wondered.

"No, I didn't have one. But everything's in my notes."

"It's always good to tape-record if possible. You can buy a little hand-held recorder pretty cheaply. That way you always have back-up," he suggested.

"Okay, I'll keep that in mind." But I wasn't going to rush out and spend money on a tape recorder. My notes were good enough.

"You about done? I'm afraid I have to lock up the news-room," McCloud said at around 4:30.

"Uh-huh. I'm just proofreading it now."

"The *Herald*'s deadline isn't until next week, you know," he pointed out.

"I know, but I want to get this in early. Thanks for keeping the room open."

"No problem, Jason. I'm always here until at least 4 every day. I never know who might pop in to see me," McCloud said.

"Don't forget, we have a guest speaker in class on Friday," he added, whipping out his keys as we headed toward the door.

"You know Jason, you're becoming a really good reporter," McCloud said, slamming the door shut and turning his key. "I think we'll hear big things from you in the future."

CHAPTER 5

Miles Cannon sauntered into the room like he was a king. Then he hit play on the TV set positioned in the front of our journalism class. The tape rolled.

"AND NOW, THE NIGHTLY NEWS WITH MILES CANNON ..."

I glanced back and saw Julie rolling her eyes.

Cannon wore an expensive-looking pinstriped suit with a red handkerchief in the front pocket and shoes polished to a glossy shine. His hair was full and black on top but grey around the temples. The way black met grey, and then thinned out, it looked suspiciously like a toupee.

"For any of you who might not know me from News Channel 4, I'm Miles Cannon," he announced, like a royal proclamation.

"Today I'm going to teach you how the professionals do their job," he said in a condescending tone. "I've been in this news business for 25 years, and I've reported on all kinds of stories. There isn't much Miles hasn't seen."

"On a teleprompter," I heard Julie mutter from the back.

Miles proceeded to sell himself for the next 20 minutes, telling us how cool and calm he was broadcasting on 9/11 and how many Emmy awards News Channel 4 had won with him as anchor.

"I said to everybody right when we caught Osama bin Laden, 'I knew he was in Pakistan all along,' " he claimed. "I smelled it from the start."

Somehow, I was skeptical of that. Even though he'd mastered the concerned look of a television anchorman, Cannon's brown eyes communicated insincerity.

He dropped plenty of names, too, telling us how he'd interviewed everyone from Lady Gaga to President Obama.

"One time Derek Jeter mentioned to me that he felt uncomfortable at the plate against a certain pitcher," Cannon said. "I suggested to him off camera that he stand a little deeper in the batter's box. The next night he got a triple."

I dropped my head and shook it slowly. Oh, please, now you're Derek Jeter's batting coach!

"Being a TV newsman isn't for everyone," he said, wrapping up his speech. "There's a lot of pressure, and frankly, many people can't handle it. It's an extremely important job. I always keep in mind that I'm a vital link to the public, providing them with the information they need to know. That's what keeps me going, the public's right to know.

"Now, I'll be happy to entertain any questions."

I felt like asking, "How did you become so arrogant?" But Tara Brantley's hand shot up first.

"Who would you pick as your favorite interview?" she shouted out. Talk about a softball question.

"That's hard to say ... I've interviewed so many great ones," Cannon said. "Maybe Obama. I got the man when he was an Illinois senator. It was fun to match intellects."

"How do you break into the field of television news?" someone else asked.

"The best way is to start at a small station as an intern and work your way up. I started in Fresno, California."

"Were you an intern there?"

"Not exactly. I had a contact who recommended me for a news writing position. I was only 24 at the time, and they saw potential in me. Before you knew it, I was hired in San Francisco, and then Chicago came calling."

"Did News Channel 4 really go out to San Francisco and ask you to be their anchor?"

"Well ... no, I sent them an audition tape. I was working in front of the camera by then and a friend of mine put in a word for me in Chicago," Cannon said.

"Any more questions for our guest?" Mr. McCloud asked. Maybe even he was getting tired of Cannon's act.

"Yes," I jumped in, seeing my opening. "What do you think is causing the declining ratings of network news?"

Cannon's face tightened, baring the lines that make-up probably concealed when he was on camera.

"Not all network newscasts have fallen in the ratings," he said, clearly annoyed at the question. "That's generalizing, and a good journalist doesn't do that."

"So yours haven't?" I asked.

"Our ratings have dropped some," he grudgingly admit-ted, "but that's to be expected with cable news stealing viewers and the Internet giving it out for free 24/7. It's an unfair advantage."

I followed up with, "Do you think network news has a future?"

"Of course it has a future!" he fired back. "Is that the last question?"

"I just have one more," I blurted out, despite his grow-ing impatience. "Since Woodward and Bernstein uncovered Watergate it seems like investigative reporting has faded away. Do you see that happening at your station?"

"Have you ever watched News Channel 4? Have you?" he snapped back.

"I've seen it a few times," I said, lying through my teeth.

"Then you should know we've done plenty of investiga-tions over the years. Why, just last year I broke the story on credit card scams in our area."

"How did you get that one?" I wondered.

"Our team of News Channel 4 reporters got it! But I broke it to the public."

By now Miles Cannon looked pretty ticked off, so Mr. McCloud jumped in. "Let's give Mr. Cannon our thanks for taking time out from his busy schedule to speak to us today," he said. "I think we all learned a lot."

Yeah, that he has an ego the size of Jupiter, I thought to myself.

"Boy, he sure didn't like the questions you were asking," Julie said to me as class broke up.

"Yeah, and then he tried to embarrass me. Was he arrogant or what? The great Miles Cannon — hah!"

I made a pledge to myself. Someday, I was going to beat that guy on a story.

CHAPTER 6

A week later, I was in the lunchroom eating my ham sand-wich and gulping my Pepsi when I heard a familiar thud. "Paper's in!" I announced to the table without hesitation.

I rushed over as a deliveryman dropped large bundles of the *Herald* onto a vacant table. He used a box cutter to sever the plastic straps binding copies together.

As a freshman I wouldn't have paid any attention to a new edition of the *Herald* being delivered, but now it was an event in my life. I grabbed three copies off the top of one bundle and sped back to my food. Some other kids followed me to the delivery table — although it wasn't exactly a stampede.

"Check out my story in sports, guys," I said to Max and Kevin, my lunch buddies. While they fumbled through the sections, I got there first. The headline jumped right out:

Cruz: Eagles should be nationally ranked

"Wow, he said that?" Max said after finding the page.

"Well ... not exactly." My eyes continued to scan the sto-ry. "He said we deserve votes for a national ranking."

"What's the difference?" Kevin chimed in.

"It's like the difference between getting votes for Home-coming king and actually being Homecoming king," I replied, my eyes buried in the newspaper.

"Hey, Cruz really trashes Greg Maxwell in this," Max said. "Look at what he says: 'Maxwell makes the tackle because I'm double-teamed. He's overrated.' Whoa, that's cold!"

"Yeah, how could you write this about your friend?" Kevin added.

"Keep reading, I stick up for him," I pointed out.

"Oh yeah, 'However, facts don't lie. Maxwell leads the team in tackles and is considered by some to be the better linebacker.' Good point, Jason. Take that Pete!" Kevin said, before taking another bite of his cinnamon raisin bagel.

"This is a great story. Cruz really shoots his mouth off," Max said, looking over at me.

"Thanks, man."

But I had no time to bask in praise. Moments later I heard a booming voice from behind me.

"Jefferson!!!"

I turned around to see Pete Cruz approaching in a huff.

"What the hell is this crap? I didn't think you'd print everything I said!" he fumed, shoving his copy of the paper in my face like he was reprimanding a dog.

I sat there silent. I didn't know how to respond. Finally, I said, "You never said anything was off the record."

"What the hell does that mean?"

"You never said that anything in the interview was not for print."

"The stuff about Maxwell was!" Cruz roared. "I said it in private!"

"But you saw me writing it down."

"Yeah, but I didn't think you'd use it!"

"I *never* heard you say it was off the record."

"Then you need to get your hearing checked! I must've said something!"

At that point, I was afraid Cruz was going to haul off and belt me. I braced myself as I looked up at his furious face.

"What are you so mad about, the stuff about the national ranking? The part about you being the best player in the state?" I cautiously probed.

"Nah, I don't care about that," Cruz said, showing a slight sign of softening. "It's the other stuff about Maxwell. It could get me in hot water with Coach and mess up team spirit. That's what bothers me!"

"Sorry," I offered. But I had no idea why I was apologizing. I reported the story accurately.

The story caused a stir, just like I thought it would. People kept coming up to me in school, commenting on it.

"You give me a reason to pick up the *Herald*," said one kid. "You get the real scoop."

Others told me what they thought of Pete Cruz. "Boy, he really comes off as a jerk," a guy from my Spanish class said. "Pretty cocky. The team's really good, but there's no way we should be nationally ranked with those football factories in Florida and Texas."

"Maybe not," I replied. "But the team is pretty awesome. I don't see anyone beating us in Illinois."

But the one person I wanted a reaction from was Greg. What did he think about Pete's comments about him? I didn't run into Greg that day. Was he trying to avoid me? Hadn't he read the story yet? I didn't know.

After school that day, I strode triumphantly into the *Herald* newsroom, knowing without a doubt that my sports story was going to be the best-read article in the latest edition.

"Hey, Scoop!" Julie greeted me. Other reporters congratulated me too, or at least smiled in a respectful way. A few, probably jealous, ignored me.

Gina Giantoli sure didn't ignore me.

"Jefferson, get over here. I need to talk to you," she demanded, ushering me over to her computer. I could tell by the way that she called me 'Jefferson' that she wasn't a happy camper. When she liked what I wrote she called me by my first name.

"How in the world could you write that stuff? Pete Cruz was all over me this afternoon, saying he was misquoted. We may have to print a retraction."

"Gina, he said every word of it," I fired back, confidently.

"Maybe he did, but he says the stuff about Maxwell was all off the record. And you printed it!"

"I swear, he never told me it was off the record. He's lying to cover his butt."

Gina stared at me like she wasn't sure whom to believe, but she wasn't leaping to my defense.

"You're new here. You need to be very careful quoting people," she stressed.

"I am. I got this right. I swear I did!" By now other kids were eavesdropping on the conversation.

"It's not just the quotes. You injected your opinion into the story again. You can't say, 'Maxwell is considered by some to be the better linebacker.' Who's 'some'? You don't name any names. That's just you speaking."

"No it's not. I talked to Coach Dawson, and he says college scouts are higher on Greg," I countered. "He is too, but he can't come out and say it."

"Well, you should get him to say it — on the record — if you're going to write that."

"C'mon Gina, I back it up with facts ... like tackles made. And you know reporters sometimes use anonymous sources. Woodward and Bernstein did."

"You're not Woodward or Bernstein!" she screamed.

"Everybody's talking about my story. Isn't that what you want?" I pointed out.

"I want to continue to put out an award-winning school paper, not sloppy reporting!"

"It wasn't sloppy. It was accurate."

"I should be getting on Steven in sports for not editing this story better," Gina said, straightening her black-rimmed glasses. "That's what I get for not reading it myself. I guess I have to read every word of their copy, too."

"You're making too much of this, Gina," I assured.

"Just go, Jefferson," she said, flicking her hand and abruptly turning back toward her computer. "I've got my column to write."

Julie made eye contact with me as I walked away, and gave me a thumbs-up. Mr. McCloud looked up from his desk across the room and waved me over. He offered under-standing eyes and his voice didn't sound too concerned.

"Jason, remember what I told you the other day about getting a tape recorder. That way no one can ever say they were misquoted."

"Oh, he doesn't claim he was misquoted," I said. "He says it was off the record ... which it wasn't."

"Well, you'll have proof of that, too, if you tape the entire conversation," McCloud pointed out.

I left the *Herald* newsroom that day with mixed emo-tions. The story had brought me a mega dose of attention as a journalist — which was a good thing — but also flak from my editor-in-chief. And I hadn't heard anything from my friend Greg. I decided I'd go see where I stood with him.

We didn't have any of the same classes, but I knew where to find Greg. I headed over to football practice the next afternoon. It seemed strange that I hadn't heard any-thing from him, or from Sara, about the story. Was he mad at me for writing it? I couldn't imagine why he would be. I defended him in print.

I waited by the football field as the guys streamed out for practice. Before Greg came out, Pete Cruz jogged by.

"Lookin' to stir up more trouble, Jefferson?" he said with a sneer. "Why don't you get out of here." Cruz yanked on his helmet and kept moving right past me.

A minute later Greg came out of the athletic building.

"Jason. What's up, dude?" he said, giving me a firm hand-shake. Whew! Everything was cool.

"Hi, Greg, how're you doing?"

"Great! Hey, thanks for getting my back when Cruz took a shot at me. You defended me nicely in the paper."

"Sure ... I had to," I said, as he bent to tie the shoelaces on his cleats. "Has he said anything to you about the story?"

"Not a word," Greg said, straightening back up. "But then, that's the way Pete is."

"Hi, Greg." A sexy voice interrupted our conversation. It was Marla Montez. I figured she must be hanging around practice to watch her boyfriend, quarterback Rob Kelley. Kelley wasn't out of the locker room yet.

Marla could command anyone's attention. Her thick blonde hair fell past her shoulders, leading to a body with curves in all the right places. She was particularly well-endowed, and she advertised that with low-cut tops. Her jeans looked like they were spray-painted on over shapely legs and a killer butt. Guys practically drooled on the days she wore a short skirt.

As a member of the Hillsboro High Dance Team, Marla had all the moves. It figured that the quarterback would get her.

"Hi, Marla. How are you?" Greg replied, sounding a little more than friendly. "Waiting for Rob?"

"I just like watching the team practice," Marla said, smiling. "You sure are good."

I wasn't sure if she meant Greg or the entire team by that, but I watched as Greg replied, "Thanks."

"Are you going to the Homecoming dance?" she asked.

"Yeah, I am," Greg answered. "Are you going with Rob?"

Marla hesitated before answering. "Probably," she said. "I'll see you there."

Greg put on his helmet, his long brown hair poking out to his shoulder pads, and ran onto the field for stretching. I watched practice for a half hour and then left to do some rehabbing on my knee, secure in knowing that Greg and I were still solid.

CHAPTER 7

Gina started giving me the cold shoulder. I didn't get a decent assignment for nearly a month. It didn't make sense. I thought she'd be happy with the attention I brought the *Herald*, but I guess I was wrong. She acted like she didn't trust me as a reporter.

I stayed busy, though. By October, I was pretty much a regular in the school's weight room, lifting light weights to rehabilitate my knee. My doctor told me not to overdo it, but the knee would recover faster if I exercised it regularly. I couldn't wait to run again.

That's where I got to know Frederick Hall.

Frederick was the student trainer for the football team. You didn't call him Fred or Freddy, it was always Frederick.

"To maximize your physical therapy, I suggest a set of anaerobic exercises, supplemented by aerobic exercises later on," Frederick said to me one day. "You need to stick to a routine without deviating."

"Yeah, thanks Frederick ... whatever you just said. My doctor already gave me some exercises to do. You know some others?"

Frederick showed me a few more to strengthen the knee, an assortment of quad exercises, leg curls and heel raises. The next time I saw him, he had them all printed out on a piece of paper — even with little diagrams.

Frederick couldn't help me enough. He seemed to get a rush when people asked for his advice. A little guy with thick glasses and pipe-cleaner-thin arms, he struck me as someone who knew he would never be an athlete, but just liked being around them. And he was more organized than some of my teachers. On game days, Frederick could tell you exactly which players had their ankles taped. He also charted the weightlifting regimens for all of the football players.

What was really nice was he included me in that group.

"You're doing wonderful Jason. Anterior cruciates take time to mend, but I think you're ahead of schedule," he encouraged.

One Monday in the weight room, I was doing easy leg lifts when Greg walked in. His muscles bulged from under his Hillsboro Eagles T-shirt like they were about to break through the cotton.

"Hey, Jason buddy. Workin' hard?"

"Just rehabbing," I said between heavy breaths. "How about you?"

"We just got out of a film session. Thought I'd lift for a while."

I looked up from my workout bench and watched Greg rip off 10 reps on the bench press. The metal plates were stacked so high, he must have been lifting 300 pounds! The weights finally crashed back down with a clank that could probably be heard in the locker room as Greg let out a primal scream. "Ahhhhh!"

Just then Pete Cruz walked in. He took one look at the two of us and quickly turned away.

"You gonna be on that long?" he asked Greg, turning back around.

"No, take it Pete," Greg answered, moving on to the leg machine.

From that point on it almost seemed like a competition, but Pete always lagged a little behind. Greg handled heavier weights and more repetitions.

But I don't think Greg was trying to compete or show off. He was just naturally stronger. It was probably his usual routine. Pete, on other hand, never lowered the weight when he moved onto a machine that Greg had just used. He strained to do fewer reps.

"Practice has been moved up to 3:30 tomorrow," Pete called out as he was about to leave the weight room. "Coach wants the offense to work on a few new plays."

"Yeah, thanks Pete, I know," Greg replied.

With Pete gone, our conversation picked up again.

"They're expecting a huge crowd for Homecoming Saturday," I pointed out. "I think everybody's coming back to see you guys play."

"Is that right? The more fans the better," Greg said, reaching for a towel.

"I can't believe it. You guys have still only given up one touchdown all season."

"That's right, and it's our goal not to give up another."

"Are you and Sara going to the dance?"

Greg hesitated before responding. "Maybe," he said. "You going?"

"Well, I don't know how much dancing I'll do, but I'll be there. I can always dee-jay if the music is lame."

Greg smiled back at me and wiped the sweat off his forehead and arms. "I expect to see you break-dancing."

———

"Wow, there must be 10,000 people here," I said to Max as we squeezed into the stands at the Homecoming game. Max zipped his coat all the way up over his broad stomach and pulled out his wallet as our butts met the cold, hard metal seats. The school band, seated to our right, blasted out their version of "Fly Like an Eagle" and the tempting scent of charcoal-grilled pretzels wafted through the air.

"Remind me to get one of those big pretzels at halftime," Max said. "We won't be able to get out of our seats until then."

"This could get ugly," I remarked, shouting over the band. "Evanston has only won two games all season."

"I know. That's why we've got them for Homecoming," Max said with a laugh. "You always pick an opponent you can beat."

"This year, they could pick anyone," I said. I pulled out my wool hat to cover my buzz-cut hair.

Sure enough, the game was never in doubt. Our defense was so dominant, every time Evanston snapped the ball, our guys blew across the line of scrimmage like convicts on a jail break. The poor quarterback barely had time to move. I heard some old guy in the stands tell his wife that Hillsboro's defense looked like the 1985 Chicago Bears.

Greg was all over the field. He must have had 15 tackles. Cruz had plenty of tackles too, plus a fumble recovery and an interception, which he returned 30 yards for a touchdown. I couldn't imagine a better pair of high school linebackers.

Evanston managed 50 yards of total offense, at best. I don't know if they even had positive rushing yards.

Offensively, it seemed like any play we called worked. I was right, the final score was ugly. We won 48-0.

"That's 9-0 now — conference champions and an undefeated regular season. Time to get ready for the state playoffs," I said to Max.

"Yeah, I think I'll celebrate with another one of those pretzels — if they're still selling them," Max replied.

"Go now, and I'll catch up," I said. "I'm going to wait so I don't have to battle the crowd going out."

Just then the band broke into "We are the Champions." I ached to be a player again, on the field celebrating.

That night, Kevin met up with us for the Homecoming dance.

"Hey, Max. Hey, Scoop, over here!" he yelled, greeting us outside the gym. It wasn't easy picking Kevin out in a crowd. He stood about 5-foot-7 and his face was sort of nondescript.

The place was decorated with blue and gold stream-ers — the school colors — and as soon as we walked in we heard the rock band playing "We are the Champions."

"That's getting to be our unofficial theme song," I said to the guys.

We got some punch and wedged our way through the crowd to an opening just under one of the football banners.

"You guys going to dance tonight?" I asked.

Kevin craned his neck. "I'm checking out the talent. You never know. If Marla Montez comes over and asks me, I sure wouldn't turn her down."

"You'll have to get past Greg Maxwell first," Max said.

"What?" My eyes darted over to Max.

"Look over there," he said, pointing. "He's got his arm around Marla."

I couldn't believe my eyes. Where was Sara?

"What's Greg doing out with Marla?" I wondered aloud.

Just then Julie Briscoe popped by and grabbed my hand. She was dressed like a hippie as usual, with an embroidered peasant top and a free-flowing flowered skirt. I had to admit, though, she looked kind of cute.

"C'mon Jason, let's dance," she said, tugging my hand.

"Uh, Julie, are you forgetting something," I said, pointing to my knee.

"Oh, just dance slow. You don't have to move much."

I really wasn't wild about the idea, but Julie was persis-tent. And she was a friend. I followed her out to the dance floor, while Kevin and Max shouted after me.

"Wo-o-o-o! You go Twinkletoes!"

While I basically stood in place and moved my hips a little, Julie twirled around wildly, waving her arms through the air. Her long brown hair flowed in every direction and her skirt flew up like a parachute as she spun about.

"You've got an *interesting* style of dancing," I pointed out, choosing my words carefully so as not to hurt her feelings. I really thought she danced like someone on bad mushrooms.

"Thanks! You've got to get into the music and let it take you away."

I just smiled back. My mind was really on something else.

"Julie, did Greg break up with Sara Cooley?" I asked when the dance mercifully ended.

"You haven't heard? Yeah, he's with Marla now. Sara's not too happy about it, from what I understand."

"I can't believe that," I said. "They've been going together forever."

"I guess he found someone he likes better," Julie said, brushing it off like just another Hollywood romance.

"Well, I feel sorry for Sara," I said. "Besides, I thought Marla was going with Rob Kelley."

"Not anymore," Julie said.

"I'm going to go get something to drink. See you later, Julie."

"Bye!"

But I detoured on my way to the refreshment table to say hello to Greg. Maybe it was my reporter's instinct, wanting to get the straight scoop.

"Jason, how are ya? I saw you out there dancing," Greg said, greeting me warmly.

"Yeah, if you can call it that," I said. He must have seen my eyes travel over to Marla, who was looking as sexy as ever in one of her miniskirts.

"You know Marla, right?"

"Not really. Hi, Marla."

"You write for the school paper, don't you?" Marla asked.

"Yeah, I do. Sometimes I cover the football team." Actually, I had only written one story on the team — the famous Pete Cruz feature — but I was looking to do more.

"Jason and I are from the same neighborhood," Greg pointed out to Marla. "We used to play a lot of wild games without pads. Remember that day it started pouring and we kept playing in the mud?"

"Yeah, it was great. We slid 20 feet on every tackle. I came home covered in mud."

"Jason would be on the team now if he didn't hurt his knee in spring practice," Greg said to Marla.

"Bummer," she replied.

We talked for a minute before I headed off to the refreshment table. The line was so long, I wondered if somebody had spiked the punch. After 10 minutes, I was just about to the front of the line when I heard a commotion from across the room. People were really yelling, so I got out of line and rushed over to see what was going on.

That's when I saw two or three guys trying to hold back Greg. He was hopping mad about something, and it looked like Marla was trying to calm him down. The last time I saw Greg so angry was when Billy Esposito blindsided him in one of our neighborhood tackle games and then claimed it was a legal block. He was going berserk.

I hurried over to Max and Kevin. "What happened?" I asked.

"I don't know. Greg went nuts on Rob Kelley, gave him a big shove and knocked him down," Kevin said. "I just caught part of it."

"I don't think he liked Rob talking to Marla," added Max. "Maybe Kelley was trying to win her back."

Mr. Barnes, the science teacher who was acting as a chaperon, and a police officer were soon on the scene, quieting Greg down. Rob was jawing right back, and Greg had to be restrained.

"I'm going over there to check it out," Kevin said, starting off across the gym floor. "You coming?"

"No, I want to give Greg some space," I replied.

"You sure?" Kevin called back. "It might be a good story for the paper." I waved him off.

Max turned to me and remarked, "Those football guys are sick! They may be undefeated, but they sure don't get along."

CHAPTER 8

A few weeks after Homecoming, I cruised into the *Herald* newsroom after school to see if Steven had any more sports stories for me. My knee was feeling a lot better after weeks of physical therapy, including Frederick Hall's exercises. Pretty soon I was going to start jogging.

"Jason, you've got something in the mail box," Gina said as soon as I entered the room. She was busy opening up her own mail.

I walked over to my mail slot in the shelf on the wall. Inside was a white envelope that just read "Jason Jefferson" on it. Strangely, it was typed. I opened it up. Inside was a plain sheet of white paper printed from a computer.

There's something serious going on with the football team. You need to investigate.

That's all that was on the paper, except one other thing. It was signed "**Deep Throat.**"

I read the note a second time and then smiled. All right, someone was playing with me. Someone was busting my chops.

"Very funny, Gina," I called over to her, waving the paper. "This was you, right?"

"Jefferson, I don't know what you're talking about." If that was her poker face, it was a good one.

"This note? You didn't send it?"

"No. It was just in the newspaper's pile, and I sorted mail today."

"Yeah, sure. Well, if it wasn't you, somebody's playing a joke."

"Why? What does it say?"

I stopped before giving her an answer. While I was almost sure it was a joke, a speck of doubt was lodged in my mind. Could it possibly be a serious note, giving me a legitimate tip? If so, I didn't want Gina knowing about it.

"Oh, forget it," I finally said, stuffing the note in my pocket.

"You're weird, Jefferson," Gina said, shaking her head. "But I've got a story for you, if you want it. I need someone to do a feature on fashion, what kids are wearing these days."

Another lightweight story.

"No, I want to do hard news," I replied. "Besides, I want to stay in sports right now."

"Suit yourself. You can see what Steven has. But make sure your quotes are accurate this time."

"They were accurate last time!" I fired back, but she wasn't even listening.

Steven surprised me when I asked about an assignment. "I need someone to cover the state playoff game in Peoria on Friday night. You up for that?"

"You're kidding me," I said, as my jaw dropped. "We're 12-0 and in the semifinals and you don't have someone to cover it?"

"Yeah, well, it's at least a three-hour drive, and Dave said he couldn't make it."

"That doesn't matter. Put me down for it. I'm in with Coach Dawson. He'll probably let me ride on the team bus."

Over the next few days, I kept thinking about that anonymous note, but I didn't show it to a soul. Who would try to mess with me like that? I wondered if Max and Kevin were pulling a prank. I brought it up at lunch time.

"You guys are real clever with the 'Deep Throat' stuff," I remarked.

"Deep Throat? What are you talking about?" Max replied.

I could tell by his tone of voice, and the look on Kevin's face, that they were genuinely unaware of the note. To begin with, they weren't good enough actors to pull it off. Besides, they never took journalism class. I didn't think they even knew who "Deep Throat" was.

Pete Cruz might be fooling with me, after that feature he complained about. But that story was over a month ago. And why would he say something "serious" is going on with the football team? The only serious thing was the serious can of "whup-ass" they opened up on opponents.

I placed the note in my desk drawer at home, and gradually got it out of my mind.

I concentrated on my physical therapy instead, determined to be ready when spring practice rolled around. Whenever we got a decent day in November that wasn't too cold, I'd jog on the track after school. Usually, the football team didn't want anybody on the oval track surrounding the field when they practiced, but Coach Dawson never chased me off. I think he still considered me part of the team, which only made me work harder.

One late afternoon, as I was waiting in front of the school for a ride home following my workout, a familiar voice called out.

"Hi Jason. How's it going?"

I looked up. Sara Cooley sat down next to me on the wall and dropped her overstuffed backpack, which landed with a thud.

"Sara, how are you?" I was genuinely happy to see her, and have her approach me first. Since her breakup with Greg, I hadn't talked to her. It just felt too awkward.

"I'm okay, I guess," she said, the usual sparkle missing from her eyes. "I had to stay after to make up a physics exam. I was out sick all last week."

"How'd you do?"

"All right, I think. How's your knee these days?"

"Getting stronger all the time. I'm running now."

"That's great!" she said with a warm smile.

There was a brief lapse in conversation, and then I looked at her. "Hey, I'm sorry about you and Greg."

Her brown eyes darted away. "Yeah, well, everybody breaks up eventually. I guess it was our time."

"I'm sorry," I repeated. "I know just how you feel."

"How could you? You're not a girl, and you've never broken up with somebody."

"No, but believe me, I know. I've been abandoned too."

Sara stared at me, a bit puzzled. "Did Greg ever say anything to you about us?" she asked.

"No. Why? I always thought you guys would never break up. You were great together."

"We were, and I still have feelings for him. But he's gotten kind of moody. I never could figure out what was going on."

"Maybe it's the pressure of football and college recruiting," I suggested.

"I don't know. I gave him back his varsity letter jacket. He seems to be happy with Maaar-la" Sara said, dragging out the name and rolling her eyes. "But I heard he almost got into a fight at the Homecoming dance."

"Yeah, I was there. I think Rob was hitting on her again."

"Oh? Well, I just want Greg to be happy. Tell him I said so," Sara said.

Honk!

"There's my ride. See you, Jason."

———

The team looked loose but focused as we boarded the bus for the ride to Peoria and the state semifinals. I sat up front with Frederick, the student-trainer. We left plenty early for the 7 p.m. game. I even skipped seventh period.

"What's the scouting report on Peoria? Have you heard anything?" Frederick asked me, as the bus pulled away.

"They've got a real good quarterback," I said. "I think he's thrown 20 touchdown passes and run for 800 yards this season. They run the triple option. At least, that's what I read online."

"Really? We've only played one option team this year, Danville," Frederick noted.

"Yeah, but we handled them okay. And I'm sure Peoria's never seen a defense like ours. I was doing the math. When you add in the state playoff wins against Batavia, Lake Forest and Crystal Lake, we've outscored teams 306 to 21 this season. That's incredible!"

Just then Coach Dawson butted in. "Frederick, you remembered the first-aid kit didn't you?"

"Yes Coach."

"That's what I thought. Just checking," Dawson said with a smile. "I can always count on you."

He sat back down, and Frederick and I kept talking. I actually picked up some insider stuff that I could use in my game story, even though I didn't write it down. Pulling out a notebook, I thought, would only stifle our conversation.

"Kelley has a slightly sprained knee," Frederick revealed. "He had a brace on it in practice this week, but he may go without it tonight."

"Interesting," I said. I was wondering if Kelley hurt the knee when Greg knocked him down at the dance.

"We've got a trick play we've been working on, too, but we haven't used it in a game yet."

"No kidding! What kind of play?"

"It's like a Statue of Liberty play where Kelley fakes like he's throwing, but Marques Caldwell takes a handoff on a reverse and runs around left end. Marques is *really* fast."

"You think we'll see it tonight?"

"I don't know. Maybe."

When you're on a bus sitting next to someone for three hours you learn a lot about them. You start to sense if that person is hiding something or, worse, a liar. Frederick didn't strike me as either. He was a straight-shooter.

"Frederick, is anything going on with the football team that could be considered ... well ... serious?" I asked.

"What do you mean?"

"I don't know, maybe something that's kind of ... uh, troublesome?" Now I was beginning to feel uncomfortable. It seemed like a crazy, unfounded question. After all, the note was probably a hoax.

"No. Why?"

"Oh, nevermind."

Frederick seemed to know everything that was going on with the Hillsboro Eagles. I was sure he would have told me if something bad was going on.

When we arrived in Peoria the sun was going down, and I parted ways with the team. The players put on their shoulder pads and headed onto the field for warm-ups, while I slowly climbed up to the press box, located about 30 feet above the stands. I knew that when the game ended, I'd have to move quickly, first grabbing the opposing coach for quotes, all the while keeping my eye on the bus. I figured there would be plenty of time to interview Coach Dawson and our players on the long ride home. But I sure didn't want to be left stranded in Peoria.

The game began, and I couldn't believe my eyes. Peoria took the opening kickoff, and on the second play from scrimmage, their quarterback faked a pitchout and darted

68 yards for a touchdown. It looked like our defensive end was totally faked out, playing the pitch man, and neither Greg nor Pete could make the tackle from their linebacker spots. The guy was quick as lightning.

The Peoria fans were going nuts, while our fans looked stunned. All of a sudden, we were down 7-0 — the first time we'd trailed all season!

After the extra point I looked down at the sidelines. Cruz was yelling at the defensive players, trying to get them fired up.

Our offense stalled on its first two drives. We were in for a ball game, that's for sure, not the usual romp Hillsboro was accustomed to. Peoria's option offense kept ripping off nice chunks of yardage — five to 10 yards at a time. Our guys couldn't figure out how to stop it. The quarterback — Ellison was his name — was like a slippery eel no one could lay a hand on.

But every time Peoria drove into our territory, the defense found some way to hold them off. Twice Peoria fumbled, and one other time Greg and Pete formed a brick wall, stopping their fullback cold on fourth-and-two at the Hillsboro 38.

With 3:44 left in the half, our offense broke through. Kelley hit Curtis Jones on a 20-yard touchdown pass, pulling us even at halftime.

I texted Max and Kevin: "Can U b leve we're tied 7-7?"

I couldn't. Peoria's option offense was uncovering some chinks in our armor. For the first time all season, the defense didn't look impenetrable.

Call it good coaching, call it determination, or call it pride, but the defense made the right adjustments in the second half. Peoria still managed a couple of big runs, but overall, their bucking-bronco offense was corralled. Guys started blanketing the pitch man, cutting off the option, and laying some nasty hits on Ellison.

We grabbed the lead when Cruz, playing fullback, slammed in from three yards out, and a 30-yard field goal put Hillsboro ahead 17-7 at the end of the third quarter. By that time, the way the defense was revived, I knew we were destined for the University of Illinois, site of the finals.

Peoria came up with one more big play. They put their best athlete, Ellison, back on kick returns, and the quicksilver quarterback ran back a punt 55 yards for a touchdown with four minutes left in the game. But it wasn't enough. Final score: Hillsboro 17, Peoria 14. On to the state finals!

The bus was rocking as everyone grabbed their seat for the ride home. A foot-stomping chant of "Hills-boro Ea-gles, Hills-boro Ea-gles" broke out, led by the cheerleaders surrounding the bus outside. Cruz ripped off his shoulder pads and let out a scream like Tarzan.

Just as the bus pulled away from the field, Coach Dawson stood up, cell phone in hand. He turned to face the back of the bus.

"All right, listen up!" he called out, as one of his assistant coaches blew his shrill whistle.

"I don't know if I needed that, Coach, but thanks," Dawson said, as everyone around him chuckled.

"I just got a call from the Rockford semifinal. Rockford beat Wheaton 35-28. We've got them in the finals. It's on to Champaign, baby!"

The bus erupted in joyous screams. As I looked around at all the smiling faces, I thought about the anonymous note, and I wondered to myself: How could anything on this team possibly be wrong?

CHAPTER 9

On Monday, I headed into the *Herald* newsroom right after school to see the sports editor. As I walked through the door, Rob Kelley was coming out.

"Hey, great win against Peoria," I said. "You guys really hung in there."

Kelley nodded back.

"How's your knee, Rob?"

"All right," he answered. By this time I was looking at Kelley's back. He seemed in a hurry, for some reason.

"They're kicking ass, man!" Steven said, as soon as he saw me. He rose from his desk to deliver a high-five. "State championship game!"

"Yeah, but the last one wasn't so easy. Their quarterback was awesome. He ..."

Steven cut me off before I could deliver any more game analysis. "Hey, I've got you down for the final game in Champaign. You up for that?"

"Of course, man. I wouldn't miss it."

"Good. Dave's going too, and I told him he could do the game story, but you can do a sidebar."

"You mean a feature off the game? Sure, I'll do it."

"Cool. Maybe the team will let you ride with them again," Steven said. "If not, the school has ordered four buses for fans. There's a pep rally on Friday, the day before the game."

"I know, I heard. People are stoked," I said.

"As far as deadlines go, we can get the championship game stories into our next issue, because it doesn't close until Nov. 30. But you have to include the writeup on the Peoria game too. Keep that one shorter. It'll be old news by then."

"Got ya. Do you think I can write a column about the team when the season's over? I've got some great inside stuff I haven't used yet."

"Maybe. I'll see how our space is."

"By the way," I remarked, "what was Kelley doing in here?"

"I don't know. I didn't talk to him. He wasn't here long," Steven said.

I was about to head to the track to do my jogging, but my eyes drifted over to the mail shelf. There was something in my slot.

It was another suspicious-looking white envelope, with "Jason Jefferson" typed on the front. I ripped it open.

The football team has a serious problem. You need to investigate.

Signed,

"Deep Throat"

My eyes were glued to the note, as my mind took flight. Who could be writing these?

I couldn't keep this to myself. I needed to see what somebody else thought. But certainly not Gina, seated over at the computer bank, working feverishly. Not even Steven. No, the one person I felt I could trust was sitting 10 feet away wearing jeans and a tie-dyed hippie shirt, writing her own story. I slipped the note into my backpack and walked over to my favorite cub reporter.

"Hi flower child," I said.

Julie looked up and gave me an easy smile. "Miles Cannon! What's up?" After Cannon's visit to our classroom — and our little confrontation—she occasionally called me that as a joke.

"I need to talk to you for a second — outside," I said, motioning to the door.

"Sure." Julie looked caught off guard as we slipped out into the hallway.

"I've got to show you something," I said, whipping out the piece of paper. "I'm getting these weird notes, and I don't know what to make of them."

Julie examined the note. "Wow! It's signed Deep Throat, like from 'All the President's Men,' " she said, her eyes widening.

"Yeah, it's freaky."

"Did you know that 'Deep Throat' got his nickname from a porn movie?" Julie remarked, looking up at me.

"No, but that doesn't matter right now. What do you think of the note? Should I take it seriously?"

"Did you say you've gotten more than one note?"

"Yeah, this is the second one. The other one was exactly the same, except it just said something serious was happening. This one calls it a 'serious problem.'

"Do you think someone's playing a prank on me?"

Julie examined the note some more. "They could be. But maybe something bad is going on with the team. I don't know."

"I was thinking it had to be written by someone taking journalism class. How else would they know about Deep Throat?" I pointed out. "But who would do that? And what could they possibly know about the team?"

"Whoever it is tried really hard not to be identified. There's not even any handwriting. It's typed," Julie noted.

"I know. Why can't they just tell me face to face?"

Julie paused for a minute. "Have you investigated yet? Have you found anything bad going on with the team?"

"Nothing so far. I didn't really take the note seriously. Maybe I should look harder."

"I would. It looks like somebody's concerned. I mean, it *could* be a hoax, but I don't think so. If it were, they probably would have come clean by now."

"I know. Thanks Julie, but please don't tell anybody about this."

"Oh, I won't," she promised, before grabbing her long hair and swinging it around in front to dust my face. "I thought you wanted to talk in private to ask me out."

CHAPTER 10

"Greg, wait up!"
I didn't know if I'd get the straight scoop, but I had to at least try. After all, Greg and I were friends. He might tell me if something wasn't right with the team.

"Hi Marla," I said, cornering the lovebirds in the school hallway between classes. I noticed that Marla was wearing Greg's letter jacket — the one Sara used to wear.

"Hi Jason," she replied, giving me a nice smile.

"Greg, I need to ask you something about the team," I said, catching my breath.

"I'm going to be late for class. I'll see you later, Greg," Marla said, giving him a quick peck on the lips.

"Yeah, good luck on your math test. I'll see you at lunch, babe." He watched with adoring, puppy-dog eyes as she hurried off down the hall.

"What's up? I've got to go too."

"Hey, is anything going on with the team that's not right?

Greg looked surprised by the question. "No, everything's great. We're just getting ready for Rockford on Saturday," he said, looking serious.

"I heard something might be going on. Is anybody flunking off? Everybody's eligible to play, right?"

Greg's face loosened into a smile. "Some of our guys aren't the brightest bulbs, but they're okay to play, as far as I know."

"Because you have to have at least a C average to be eligible for sports," I pointed out.

"Yeah, I know. Some of our linemen pay off a few teachers for that," he said with a laugh.

"But you don't know for sure of any serious problems on the team, right?"

"Hell no, things couldn't be better. We're about to become state champions. I don't know why you'd think there's a problem."

"Well, I saw you knock Kelley down at the Homecoming dance."

"That's over. He gets it now. Marla's my girl."

"Yeah, I know. But why'd you break up with Sara? You guys were together so long."

Greg looked a little uncomfortable.

"Jason, Sara's a great girl. No doubt about it. But our relationship changed. And I never thought I'd hook up with someone like Marla. She's major league. What can I say? It just happened. People don't know; there's a lot more to Marla than just a gorgeous face and body. She really cares about me too."

Greg shook his shoulders to straighten his backpack. "I gotta run. You riding the bus to the game again this week?"

"Uh-huh. Good luck. I know you're going to be state champs. You guys are the best."

"Thanks." Greg patted me on the shoulder and dashed off, looking like he was in search of a ballcarrier to tackle, not a classroom.

I kept thinking about my conversation with Greg as the week wore on. He joked about some of the linemen having to pay off teachers to remain eligible; that couldn't happen, I was sure. But what about teachers voluntarily fixing the grades for football players? A possibility. I'd heard of it happening in college, why not in high school?

All of the teachers at Hillsboro High seemed honest, but most were strong supporters of the football team too. Would any of them change a D to a C to keep the Eagle powerhouse rolling? Was there a serious grade-fixing scandal under my nose?

Bob Woodward would have at least investigated the possibility. He would have asked questions. I needed to too.

The only problem was, where would I uncover that kind of information? Unless 'Deep Throat' was a teacher, and willing to talk to me, I had nowhere to turn.

I decided to see what I could uncover. When I had some free time, I headed down to the school's main office.

"Can I help you?" asked the secretary, Mrs. Polansky.

"Yes, I'm Jason Jefferson and I'm a reporter for the Herald," I said, trying to make it sound like official business. "We're doing a story on the academic standing of some of the football players, and I want to get some of their grades."

Mrs. Polansky looked at me like I had just asked for her credit card number. "You want to know the grades of other students?" she said slowly.

"Yes."

"Jason, that's confidential. I can't tell you other people's grades under any circumstances. It's against the law."

"Oh, it is?"

"Yes. I'm sure you wouldn't want others to know your grades, would you?"

"No, I guess not."

"Did Mr. McCloud assign you this story?"

"Uh ... no, I'm kind of doing it on my own."

"I didn't think so. All of the teachers are well aware of student privacy issues."

I slipped out of the main office, not daring to linger any longer. If the trouble on the team was fixed grades, I didn't see how I could ever prove it. That information was "classified," like what Woodward and Bernstein ran up against. And no one on the team was going to voluntarily show me their grades. That was for sure.

Then again, maybe I was barking up the wrong tree. Maybe the "serious problem" had nothing to do with grades. But what?

———

I nestled into the same seat next to Frederick on the ride up to the University of Illinois for Saturday's state championship game. The late November day was brisk but really pretty nice—clear skies and temperatures in the mid-30s, without much wind.

"What did you think of the pep rally yesterday?" Frederick asked me.

"It was awesome," I replied, shifting my cramped leg to make it more comfortable against the seat back. "Everybody's stoked. Look at all the fans who are going."

Outside the four buses, parked behind the bus transporting the school band, were filling fast. Together they formed a yellow caravan that would follow us to Champaign. A lot of kids brought these long blue plastic horns that could blast ear-shattering sound. I nudged Frederick and pointed to them.

"I feel sorry for the bus drivers. I hope they have headphones."

With us in the lead, the six-bus caravan started rolling for Champaign and the 1 p.m. kickoff.

"How's your knee these days?" Frederick asked.

"A lot better. I'm jogging, and I can almost run flat out. It's getting stronger every day," I replied.

"Keep it up," Frederick said, "and you'll be ready for spring practice."

"Those exercises you showed me have helped a lot, Frederick. Thanks."

"That's what I'm here for," he said with a look of appreciation.

It seemed like a good time to revisit a past conversation. "Frederick, any problems with the team? Anything new?"

This time he thought for a minute before dismissing the question outright. "The only thing wrong with this team is some of the guys don't get along. But that's not that unusual, I don't think. Whenever you have a great team with several great players, there can be petty jealousies."

"You mean like Pete and Greg?" I asked.

"Right. I think Pete wants it to be his team, and Greg is starting to get more and more of the glory."

"They should both be all-state this year," I pointed out.

"Definitely," Frederick responded. "I haven't seen any linebackers who are better."

I glanced behind me. Greg and Pete were sitting on opposite sides of the bus, well apart.

I started to think that maybe the "serious problem" on the team was nothing more than personality clashes. Maybe "Deep Throat" was overblowing the whole situation.

Two 13-0 football teams arrived at Memorial Stadium ready to rock. While our four buses were impressive, Rockford seemed to bring just as many fans. The bands began dueling as the players warmed up.

As I grabbed a seat in the press box, I heard two radio guys doing their pregame show:

"Can the irresistible force overcome the immovable object? That's the question here today. The Rockford Warriors are averaging 35 points, while the Hillsboro Eagles are giving up fewer than three points per game. What a matchup!"

"Yes Howard, when it comes to allowing points, Hillsboro is stingier than Ebenezer Scrooge. Anchored by two outstanding linebackers, and a big, strong line, the Eagles may have the best prep defense Illinois has seen in years."

"But Rockford can sure put points on the board. Fasten your seat belts, this should be a great one!"

It was. Rockford took the opening kickoff and marched into Hillsboro territory with a series of quick slant passes that seemed to catch us off guard. Their quarterback was precision-like in his passing. As soon as the receiver made his cut, the ball was in the air. When the receiver looked back, the ball was practically in his hands.

Rockford's quarterback connected on his first five throws and had us back on our heels. Nobody had ever moved the ball on us like that! But with the ball at the Hillsboro 18-yard line, Greg stepped up as always. He must have anticipated another quick slant, and he timed it just right, breaking in front of the intended receiver to intercept the pass. Greg returned the ball to midfield before being tackled.

From there, Kelley led Hillsboro on an eight-play drive, deftly mixing runs with passes. He scored on a two-yard quarterback sneak, and it looked like we were off and running to the championship trophy.

Rockford must have had other ideas. They answered right back with a 70-yard bomb, as the receiver got our cornerback, Matt Olson, to bite on a stop-and-go pattern. Our guys looked a little shocked that they were scored on so easily. It was the longest play we'd given up all season! But Rockford was clearly an explosive team.

Then they struck again. Kelley fumbled at our 16-yard line, getting blindsided as he set up to pass. Our defense held solid, stopping Rockford for no gain on two straight plays, before their coach came up with a great call. They took advantage of our strength—our aggressiveness—and ran the ball in on a draw play.

The scoreboard read: Rockford 14, Hillsboro 7. Eagles fans looked restless.

"For the first time all season, Hillsboro is behind at half-time," announced the radio guy, a few minutes later. "The

Eagles' defense has been solid, but by no means dominating. It's fallen victim to big plays."

I wondered what was going on inside our halftime locker room. Was the bad blood starting to come out, or were they holding it together?

The second half provided the answer. The defense was not just the immovable object but an irresistible force as well, disrupting Rockford's passing attack with an array of blitzes. Pete sacked the quarterback for a 10-yard loss, but Greg provided the big play, just as he had in the first half with his interception. Early in the fourth quarter, he knifed through to smack the Rockford ballcarrier just as he was taking a handoff. I mean, he really knocked him into next week! The running back coughed up the ball, and Greg recovered it deep inside Warrior territory. Steve Taylor's five-yard sweep tied the score at 14-14. Our left tackle, Luke Skoronski, completely flattened their defensive end with a pancake block to spring Taylor.

The clock continued to wind down. Neither team could move the ball. It looked like we were headed to overtime. But Coach Dawson had a trick up his sleeve.

I'd almost forgotten about the trick play Frederick told me about on the bus ride to Peoria. When I saw it unfold, I nearly fell out of my chair.

With the ball at the Rockford 45, Kelley dropped back to pass and thrust his arm forward, like he was throwing to his right. Everyone looked downfield, but the ball never left his hand. Instead he pulled it behind his back and held it there for Marques Caldwell, who was coming around behind Kelley from the right side. Caldwell snatched the well-disguised handoff and flew around left end.

By the time anyone knew he had the ball, it was too late. Marques was in the secondary, and there was no way he was going to be caught!

On the Rockford side, I could see their head coach throw his headphones to the ground and put his hands on his waist.

With 2:12 remaining, the scoreboard read Hillsboro 21, Rockford 14. Rockford had one last chance for a comeback, but they faced a defense that was breathing fire.

First down: A running play was smothered for no gain.

Second down: Their quarterback scrambled and managed two yards before Pete drilled him into the ground.

Third down: A pass over the middle was batted down by Greg.

Fourth-and-eight, last chance: The Rockford quarterback faded back to pass. Five receivers were out on patterns, and a couple of them were open. He cocked his arm.

Then came the sea of blue and gold. A tidal wave of tacklers buried him before he could even get the pass off. Leading the charge was "The Barbarian" — Greg.

Fans blasted their blue plastic horns. The familiar chords of "We are the Champions" erupted from the school band as the final seconds ticked off.

The public address announcer grabbed his mike. "The most valuable player in today's game, as selected by the media, is ...."

"Greg Maxwell of Hillsboro."

I wondered: How come I wasn't asked to vote? Still, I couldn't have been happier with the choice.

"I'm going to do my sidebar on Greg getting MVP," I said to Dave, the reporter I was double-teaming the game with.

"Fine, I'm going to write the game story around the trick Statue of Liberty play," he said. "That was unbelievable!"

I rushed down to the field, passing Marla and the dance team. "You go Jason!" she yelled to me. "Make sure to interview Greg!"

On the field, a huge mass of players and fans were hugging and celebrating, hooting and hollering. When Greg saw me he locked me in a bear hug, squeezing like a vise and lifting me off the ground.

"Not too hard, Greg. My knee!" I warned. That reminded me of the last time he picked me up, when the knee blew out in spring practice. Only by now he'd gotten even stronger.

Greg pulled off his helmet and a huge cloud of steam rose from underneath it, making him looks like some god from Mount Olympus. Sweat glistened on a face smeared with eye black, applied to ward off the sun.

Just then Coach Dawson jogged up and handed him the gold-plated MVP trophy. "Great game, Greg. This is all yours." They hugged and Dawson patted the back of Greg's head, telling him, "You earned it."

"You were awesome, man!" I said. "How does it feel?"

"Like heaven, Jason. Like heaven."

I wish I could have bottled that moment in time — the pure euphoria, the unbridled joy. For little did I know, Hillsboro High's heaven was about to become hell.

CHAPTER 11

Two weeks after the state championship game, I was sitting in the lunchroom with Max and Kevin, thumbing through the latest edition of the *Herald*, which had just arrived a day ago.

"He had 14 tackles in that game?" Max asked, shaking his head in disbelief.

"That's what the statistician had Greg down for," I said. "But his two biggest plays were the first-half interception return and the forced fumble that set up Taylor's touchdown. That's why he deserved MVP."

"I think Marques should have gotten it," Kevin said. "He scored the winning touchdown. The Statue of Liberty call was the play of the game."

"No way," I argued. "We wouldn't have even been in the game without Greg."

"But I see you gave Cruz some credit too," Kevin pointed out, sliding his finger over to a paragraph on Pete.

"Yeah, he had 10 tackles. He played great too. The whole defense rallied once we were down. For a while, I was beginning to wonder if we would."

"Well, I guess Cruz won't come looking for you this time," Kevin remarked.

Instead, we were startled by another lunch-time visitor.

"Jason, I've got to talk to you," Julie said, flitting in like a bluebird—which she kind of looked like in her colorful outfit that day.

"What is it?"

"I've got something to show you," she said, urgency in her voice. "Can I talk to you in private?"

"Go for it, Dude," Max cracked.

Julie and I moved to one of the deserted outer tables.

"I don't usually go around stealing people's mail, but I thought you'd want to see this right away. I noticed it in your slot in Mr. McCloud's room this morning. I have no idea when or how it got there."

She pulled out a familiar-looking white envelope and passed it under the table to me, onto my lap. I looked down at it. The name Jason Jefferson was typed on the front, just like the last two.

"Wow, another one," I whispered.

I glanced back up at Julie and then started to open it, never pulling the envelope up to where others might see.

There is still a serious problem with the football team. Don't stop looking.

Signed,

"Deep Throat"

But that wasn't all. This note had a cryptic line at the end.

Herman Go Home.

I passed the note back under the table to Julie. "Look at what it ends with."

She looked down at the note. "Who's Herman? Have you been fooling everybody? Is that your real name?"

"Julie, get serious for a minute. Somebody's trying to tell me something."

"Well, why can't they just come out and say it? What's up with all this secret stuff?"

"I've been thinking about that. It's pretty clear that 'Deep Throat' is terrified about having his or her identity revealed. Why else would they send anonymous typed notes? Think about it, all forms of electronic communication are traceable—text messages, emails, Facebook, tweets. And they can't use the phone, because they're probably afraid I might recognize their voice. It looks like they're even afraid I'll recognize handwriting."

"Well, they must have access to Mr. McCloud's room."

"Maybe, maybe not. I think the newspaper's mail all goes through the main office first."

Julie looked as puzzled as I was. "Do you have any idea what the problem is?" she asked, pulling back her long brown hair.

"I thought it might be grade fixing. Maybe one of the players was ineligible and played anyway. But that's really hard to prove. I can't get access to their grades."

"Have you tried?"

"Uh huh," I nodded. "Mrs. Polansky said they're confidential."

"I thought they would be. I wouldn't want anybody knowing I'm getting a D in economics this term. Not even my parents," Julie remarked.

"Yeah ... right. Well, I don't know where to look next."

"That Herman Go Home must be some kind of a clue," she said, her brown eyes widening. "Maybe, by home, they meant look close to your own life or look back in time. Don't ask me why they'd call you Herman, though."

"I don't know either." Just then the bell rang. Julie passed me the note back, under the table, and I stuffed it into my pocket. I got up to retrieve my tray at the table where Max and Kevin were still sitting. I hadn't even had a chance to eat my dessert.

"This is kind of fun," Julie said as we got up. "We have our own little mystery to solve!"

CHAPTER 12

A few days later I was in the weight room alone, doing my leg curls and quad exercises late that afternoon. It was a rare day that I had the weight room to myself. In another few weeks, after New Year's, the place would be teeming with football players participating in voluntary off-season workouts. The word "voluntary" seemed like a joke. Coach Dawson expected everyone to be there.

I caught a glimpse of someone passing by the weight room doorway. A few seconds later that figure backtracked and was standing in the hallway looking in at me.

"Jason, I didn't know you were in here," Frederick said.

"Hi Frederick. I'm just finishing up my workout."

Frederick stepped inside and looked around. "All by yourself, huh?"

"Yeah, maybe everybody else is out doing their Christmas shopping. Me? All I want from Santa is a healthy knee."

"Looks like you're almost there," Frederick said.

"I'm close. I'm running without any pain. Thanks again for showing me the exercises."

"You're welcome. Glad I could help!"

"You really know your stuff."

"I hope to be a professional someday," Frederick remarked. "After I graduate this year I'm going to college to study to be an athletic trainer."

"Really? You'll make a good one." Then I changed the subject.

"So I hear the team is being honored at Gibson's Steakhouse for finishing No. 1 in the state poll?"

"Yeah, the Booster Club is paying for it. Pretty nice."

"You get to go too, right?" I asked.

"Oh yeah, I wouldn't miss it!"

"Sweet."

"The guys might get championship rings, too."

"Pretty cool! I just wish I hadn't gotten hurt."

"Well, I've got to go," Frederick said, waving his hand. "Be careful. You really should have someone else in here as a spotter."

"I'm almost done," I replied. Frederick turned and headed for the door. Just as he was about to walk out I stopped him.

"Hey Frederick, did anybody on the team have grade problems this year?"

"Not that I'm aware of. But I'm a trainer; I don't know everybody's grades. You'd have to ask Coach that. Why are you always asking me about problems on the team?"

"It's nothing," I replied, raising my hand in a gesture of peace. "Have a merry Christmas."

"Thanks, but for me it's Hanukkah. I'm Jewish. Ours lasts longer."

"That's a good thing," I said, smiling at him.

"Do you have a big get-together for Christmas?" Frederick wondered.

"Just me and my mom."

"Oh," Frederick said, looking at me sympathetically. "Well, have a good Christmas anyway."

I finished up my set and moved on to my final station when somebody else walked in. Pete Cruz was wearing a tank top and shorts.

I took a few steps toward him. "Hi Pete. Congratulations on making all-state."

Pete just grunted, and it didn't sound like a friendly grunt.

I was astounded to look at Cruz close-up. He looked bigger than I had ever seen him—absolutely cut. Lean and buff. He also looked like he'd gained an inch in height.

Since I praised his play in the championship game article—even though the story was mostly about Greg—I expected Pete to warm up to me.

"Have you decided on a college yet?" I inquired.

"Yeah, I have. I'm pretty sold on Oklahoma State," he said.

"I'd like to get it in the *Herald* when you're ready to announce. People are interested."

"I don't know, I got burned by you once," he fired back.

I didn't want to have to defend my handling of the feature story again. Cruz obviously regretted some of what he said in the interview and wanted to take it back. But when he saw his words in print, he took the easy way out and blamed me, saying it was off-the-record. I just let it rest.

"How're you going to do this term with your grades?" I asked.

"What's it to you?"

"Nothing. I just know that guys have to keep a C average to play."

"And you don't think I have one?! You think I won't graduate or something?!"

"I didn't say that."

"Worry about your own grades, you little maggot."

There was an awkward moment of silence before Pete spoke again.

"How's your knee?" he asked. That was an encouraging sign.

"Good. It's almost back," I replied.

"It's a shame I'm graduating," Cruz said. "I'd like to come back and tear it up for ya again."

I just looked away to avoid his icy stare. Those unfeeling eyes reminded me of a great white shark.

After I recovered from the shock of that threat, I went back to lifting.

"Stay out of my way," he warned.

There was no reason to stay any longer. I might get pounded into the ground. The clock on the wall read 5 p.m., and Cruz was being a jerk. "See you later," I said after finishing my bench press. Pete didn't answer back.

That night I studied for my geometry test. Mrs. Breland was trying to squeeze one in right before the holidays. She said she didn't want us to forget everything over the break.

Before going to bed, I flicked on the 10 o'clock version of ESPN's SportsCenter. I wanted to see how the Bulls made out, who the Bears were starting at quarterback that week, and if the Cubs had signed any free agents.

The lead story that night caught my attention.

"It will not be a happy holidays for wide receiver Jeremy Banks of the Carolina Panthers. Banks, who has 73 catches this season and 12 touchdowns, is yet another big-name athlete who has been caught with performance-enhancing drugs. ESPN's John Harrison reports that, according to multiple sources, Banks failed a league-mandated drug test and faces a five-game suspension for taking human growth hormone, better known as HGH. Neither the NFL nor the Panthers will confirm or deny the report, but Banks could be the third player suspended this year for taking performance-enhancing drugs."

I turned up the volume a little. My basset hound, Oscar, was making a huffing sound and scratching at the door to go out.

"Just a minute, boy. I'll be right there," I said.

"Now we have John Harrison live with more on this story," the sports anchor said. "John, perhaps the most famous athlete to be caught using human growth hormone is track star Marion Jones, who ultimately paid a steep price by forfeiting her five Olympic medals and serving six months in prison for lying to federal agents. But, more recently, baseball's 2011 National League MVP, Ryan Braun, tested positive for HGH. Why do athletes continue to use this drug? What does it do for them?"

"Human growth hormone breaks down fat and builds lean muscle. It helps you heal from injuries faster, which is why pro athletes are attracted to it. It works like a steroid," Harrison said. "HGH can create a muscular, toned look, height, and increases in hand size that may translate into better throwing and catching skills."

I got up to let Oscar out. After a little sniffing around, he finally went to his favorite bush to pee.

"Let's go boy. It's too cold out here," I prodded. Oscar took his sweet time.

When we got back inside, SportsCenter had moved on to NBA highlights. I probably missed any news about the Bears.

I headed to bed shortly after 10:30, taking one last look at my geometry book before climbing in. I felt pretty prepared for the next day's test. You might say I had all angles covered.

As I clicked off my table lamp and closed my eyes, the pitch-black room was dead silent. I yanked the covers up under my chin. This house is always cold, I thought, as I curled up tight.

My mind drifted off, floating between thoughts. I was almost asleep when suddenly I sprang up in bed. Could it be? I lunged to turn on the table lamp again, the sudden illumination blinding my eyes as I tumbled out of bed and rushed over to my desk drawer where the anonymous "Deep Throat" notes were stashed. Yanking open the drawer, I pulled out the top note and beat a path back to the lamp, hoping to literally shed light on the mystery. I shoved the latest note under the lamp. I needed to look at it again, although I knew exactly what it said.

Herman Go Home. The first letters were all in caps. That could only stand for one thing.

HGH!

CHAPTER 13

When morning came I awoke bleary-eyed from a rest-less sleep and charged into the den to turn on the family computer. It was slow as usual, but when I finally did reach an Internet connection I Googled "human growth hormone." I had to know more.

I furiously jotted down all the information I could find. One website said HGH abuse could lead to joint aches and increased risk of diabetes, heart disease, liver disease, sleep apnea, cancer, and bone and muscle disease. Scary!

Another article said there's debate over whether it really improves athletic performance. Yet one survey showed that 195 out of 198 elite athletes said they would take a banned drug if they were guaranteed to win an Olympic gold medal and not get caught.

Then I Googled "HGH and high school athletes." One article said that in increasing numbers high schoolers, under pressure to win a college scholarship, are turning to the drug for a competitive advantage. Interesting.

"Jason, get off the computer. You're going to miss the bus!" my mom called out. I looked up at the clock. It was almost 7:30 and I had completely blown off breakfast. The bus was coming in 10 minutes.

"Okay Mom, I'm leaving."

I kept thinking about the initials HGH all the way to school. In fact, I almost forgot I had a geometry test that day. I was pretty sure that Herman Go Home had to be a clue for HGH, but I needed to know what my confidante, Julie, thought. So I hustled over to Mr. McCloud's room before third-period journalism class. I waited outside the room for her to arrive.

"You thinking about cutting class?" Julie asked when she saw me standing in the hallway.

"Julie, I need to talk to you — alone. Can you make it over to Tony's Pizzeria after school?"

"That depends," she said coyly. "Are you buying?"

"Yeah, sure. I'll spring for a large meat-eater's pizza."

"But I'm a vegetarian. I don't eat meat."

"Then we'll get half-and-half. You can have veggies on your half."

"I don't know. What if the grease from your meat flows over and pollutes my side?"

"Quit trying to bust my chops!" I said, growing exasperated. Just then the bell rang for period three and I could see Mr. McCloud coming over to shut the door. "All right, forget pizza. Let's meet at Starbucks instead. I'll buy you a latte."

"Sounds good. So we *are* having a date," she teased.

"Call it whatever you want," I muttered as we slipped into the classroom.

Journalism class that day was all about reporter's ethics and, coincidentally, we had a lively discussion about the use of anonymous sources.

"You always want to identify your sources of information in print, unless you feel that doing so would put them in jeopardy," McCloud said. "Too many reporters these days cite unnamed sources, and that's no more legitimate than hearsay. Always try to get people to speak on the record. It protects you and strengthens your story."

I raised my hand. "But what about Woodward and Bernstein during Watergate? They used 'Deep Throat,' and he was an anonymous source?"

Mr. McCloud turned and pointed toward me. "That's a good point, Jason. But they didn't build their entire story around the 'Deep Throat' interviews. They had other sources come out on the record."

"What if you're sure the person is telling the truth but they don't want their name used?" I asked.

"You still want to use their name, if possible. Sometimes sources deliberately deceive reporters," the teacher pointed out.

I wondered, Could my 'Deep Throat' be deceiving me?

When class ended, I approached Mr. McCloud. "Can I come in and use one of the computers at lunchtime?" I pleaded.

"Okay, but you know the rules: No food or drink while you're on them."

Even though I was hungry, I dug for more information about human growth hormone at lunchtime, before signing off the computer and wolfing down my bag lunch five minutes before the bell. I thanked Mr. McCloud before heading off to my afternoon class.

"Are you working on a school report, or a story for the *Herald*?" he inquired as I was leaving.

"Just doing some research," I replied.

At 3:30 I met Julie at Starbucks downtown. I was sipping my first-ever espresso when she walked in. I waved her over to my table in the corner.

"This must be really important if we couldn't talk in school," she said as soon as she got there. "I Googled 'Herman Go Home,' you know, but all I got was the name of an episode from an old TV show, 'The Munsters.' "

"It *is* really important. Sit down," I said, pulling out a chair.

"Wait a minute. Can I get my caramel latte first?" she asked.

"Okay. Get two," I said, handing her a ten dollar bill. "This espresso stuff is nasty."

"I saw your idol on TV last night," Julie remarked, as soon as she returned.

"What?"

"Bob Woodward. He was talking about a new book he has out on Bush's presidency."

"Really? Man, I'm sorry I missed that."

I whipped out the last 'Deep Throat' correspondence. I looked around to make sure no one was within earshot of our table. "I think I've cracked the Herman Go Home code," I whispered. "It stands for HGH."

"As in?"

"Human growth hormone. It's like steroids. I bet somebody on the football team is using it."

Julie dropped her latte, nearly spilling it, and leaned in toward me. "No way. Do you really think so? Wouldn't Coach Dawson know about that?"

"Probably not. They don't do drug-testing at Hillsboro, probably because it's too expensive. I don't think many high schools do. And HGH is difficult to detect anyway."

"So you think the football players are juicing up?"

"They could be. Hey, where'd you hear that term, juicing?"

"My brother's a sports fan. He always says a baseball player is 'juiced up' when he hits a long home run."

"Well, I don't know for sure, but some of our guys may be juicing too — just like the pros."

"Maybe that's why the team crushes everybody," Julie remarked with a little shake of her head. "You're going to have to investigate and see who's 'dirty' ... that's another term I learned from my brother."

"I already suspect one guy," I said. "I saw Pete Cruz the other day and he's gotten huge. He's taller and really ripped. HGH builds muscle and helps you get taller."

"But maybe he's just going through a growth spurt. Teenagers do that, you know, especially boys."

"You're right, Julie, but I remember Coach Dawson telling me that Pete has to get bigger and stronger if he's going to play linebacker in college. I'll bet anything he's using HGH."

"He could be, but don't jump to any conclusions. Remember, he's innocent until proven guilty. You need solid proof."

"Oh, I aim to get it. One way or another, I'm going to find out. Then I'll have the biggest story to ever hit the *Hillsboro Herald*."

Julie's big brown eyes widened again. "I just thought of something! You know how in 'All the President's Men,' when Woodward and Bernstein were getting stuck during the investigation, 'Deep Throat' told them 'Follow the money'? Your motto can be 'Follow the muscles.' "

"Cute, Julie."

CHAPTER 14

"Jason, don't forget you have a doctor's appointment today. I'll pick you up after school at 3," my mom reminded as I finished my bowl of Lucky Charms Tuesday morning.

"All right Mom. How many more times do you think Dr. Spencer has to see my knee?"

"This may be the last time, if everything looks good," she said.

That afternoon we drove downtown to Dr. Spencer's office, called Orthopedics Associates. "Jason, you look like you're getting around much better," he said when I walked inside his office.

"Yeah, Dr. Spencer, my knee feels great."

"No pain?"

"No."

"Well, get up on the table and lower your pants. Let's have a look," he said.

"Try flexing the knee some. Are you still wearing the brace on it?"

"Not anymore. I'm even running," I replied. "I'm planning on getting back to football in the spring."

After examining the knee for a few more minutes, Dr. Spencer delivered the news I'd been dying to hear. "I think you *can* get back to football. The knee looks about fully recovered. I don't see any reason to take another MRI."

"That's great! I've really worked hard to rehab it," I pointed out.

"I can see you have. I bet you can't wait to rejoin your team. What a wonderful season you boys had!"

"Yeah, it was tough to watch it all from the sidelines." I hesitated for a moment before asking the question that continually weighed on my mind.

"Dr. Spencer, do you think I'll ever regain all of my speed?"

"I can't say for sure, Jason. Everyone's different. All I can say is keep trying to strengthen the knee." I tried to read his face, but it didn't betray any hidden feelings.

"Do you have any other questions for me, Jason?

I sat quiet for a moment. I didn't have any more questions about the knee, but I didn't want to squander an opportunity. I had questions about another subject. Did I dare ask them?

"Dr. Spencer," I finally said. "This may seem random, but I've got some questions about human growth hormone."

"Oh, you probably saw the report on the news about the pro football player," he said, as he filled out my chart.

"Yeah. I was wondering, Is HGH totally illegal?"

"No, it's just illegal to possess it without a prescription. HGH does have beneficial uses, you know. It accelerates growth. It's prescribed for people with dwarfism whose bodies aren't growing, and for people whose muscles are wasting from cancer or AIDS. Doctors can write a prescription for those two reasons only. Anything else is illegal."

"That's what I thought," I said, but in reality I didn't know there were any legitimate uses.

"But HGH is banned in all professional sports," the doctor quickly pointed out. "That's where the NFL player got in trouble."

"How do athletes get it illegally?" I asked.

Dr. Spencer's eyes popped up from his chart. "I hope you're not looking to acquire human growth hormone. You don't need it," he said. A chuckle followed his words, relieving my anxiety about the question.

"No, I know. I was just wondering."

"Good, because it would sacrifice your long-term health. Unfortunately, HGH is available on the black market and even over the Internet, where it's not properly policed. Then there are some so-called doctors who write fraudulent prescriptions. That's a felony, punishable to five years in jail."

"Do people shoot it up with a needle, like steroids?"

"They can, but you can also find it in pill form. I'd advise athletes to just stay away from all performance-enhancing drugs."

"Oh, I do," I said.

"I hope you're not considering HGH as a way to recover faster from your injury? Like I said, it has long-term health risks."

"I know. Don't worry, Dr. Spencer, I would never go near it."

Now I knew more about HGH. But the big obstacle remained: How was I going to prove Pete Cruz was using it?

Weeks passed, and I still felt stymied. Other than catching Cruz in the act, how was I going to prove he was using human growth hormone? I knew he had to be. His rock-hard body practically screamed steroids.

For my investigation to move forward I needed help, so I reached out to my friend Frederick.

Cornering him in school one day, I asked, "Hey Frederick, do you get to see the results when everybody takes their football physicals at the start of the season?"

Frederick looked at me peculiarly, like I was once again prying for no reason. "No, I don't see that. That information is personal."

"But you'd have to know if someone failed a physical, right?"

"Yeah, the word would filter down, but it's kept quiet as to why, unless the player says something himself. We didn't have anyone fail a physical last year."

"And you didn't hear about anyone with elevated levels of hormones or anything?"

"Elevated hormones? All teenagers have elevated hormones. Jason, I don't know what you're getting at. You've been asking me these strange questions for months now. Why?"

I was beginning to get desperate. What if I let Frederick in on my investigation? Would that ruin it? Would he leak it around school?

On the other hand, I felt like I could trust Frederick, and I needed someone on the inside to keep an eye on Cruz. I didn't know where else to turn.

I looked away and stalled for time. Frederick repeated his query, "Why are you asking me these questions?"

"Frederick, come with me," I ordered. We left the school hallway and ducked inside an empty classroom. I shut the door.

"Frederick, you know I'm a reporter for the school paper, right?"

"Right."

"Well, I've been tipped off ..." I stopped in mid-sentence. I still wasn't sure I was doing the right thing, telling the student athletic trainer what I suspected. But I took a leap of faith.

"I was tipped off a couple of months back that there's a problem on the football team. I have reason to believe someone is using human growth hormone, a performance-enhancing drug."

Frederick's jaw dropped. Then he started to laugh. "At Hillsboro? That's a pretty serious charge," he contended.

"I know it is, but I have letters suggesting that."

"From whom?"

"They're anonymous ... but I've gotten several."

"Oh, it sounds like someone's just jealous of the team's success. They're trying to shoot us down," Frederick suggested.

"Maybe, but what if it's true? You know HGH is illegal, and it has long-range health risks. Don't you want to protect the health of the players?"

"Of course I do. That's my job," he said. "That, and making sure the players are prepared to play."

"I have reason to believe that Pete Cruz is using. He may even be giving it to other guys, for all I know."

"Pete?" Frederick appeared to consider the accusation. "Well, he has gotten a lot more toned. I guess it's possible. But he also lifts like a maniac. He's always in the weight room."

"Yeah, but he's gotten taller too."

"Could be a growth spurt," Frederick suggested.

"I don't think so," I replied. "Who grows that fast?"

Frederick stood lost in thought.

"Look, I'm just asking you to keep your eyes open and let me know if you see something suspicious. And I need you to swear to me that you won't breathe a word of this to anyone else. I know I can trust you."

"Okay, I'll let you know if I see anything," Frederick nodded, straightening his sweater vest and looking away.

I felt better as we opened the door and slipped back into the hallway. Now I had a mole on the inside.

_____

CHAPTER 15

"Jefferson, are you ever going to write for news side again, or are you strictly a sportswriter now?" Gina asked me one January day in the *Herald* newsroom.

"I really consider myself sports," I replied.

"Well, I haven't seen your byline there lately," she pointed out. "Are you a slacker now?"

"No, it's just that I've got a lot on my plate. I'm weight-lifting with the football team three times a week, and I'm also working on something special."

Gina's ears perked up and she hit me up for more information, like a good reporter would. "What's so special?"

"It's just a lead I'm following. Maybe nothing will come of it."

"Well, maybe you can find time to sell an ad for us. We could use one. Chateau BowWow, that dog grooming place, just pulled out. They may be going out of business."

"That's too bad. I think we brought Oscar there once. I'll help you out if I have time," I offered. Gina turned away, giving me a skeptical look.

Selling an ad was the least of my concerns. I continued my investigation to prove that Pete Cruz was using dangerous human growth hormone, not only risking his health but cheating teammates and opponents by giving himself an unfair advantage over the competition. But aside from his bulging muscles and growth in height, I suffered from a dearth of evidence. I needed direction.

Then, one day, another mysterious note turned up in my mailbox. It was almost as if my "Deep Throat" source sensed that I was frustrated and needed another clue to go on.

I ripped the envelope open as soon as I spotted it. I didn't even care about sneaking it away to some secret spot. I had to see the new message immediately.

It read: **"Herman Go Home in the locker room"**

I looked up, stashed the note in my pocket, and pumped my fist. Yes! The place to look was the locker room. That's where I'd catch Pete red-handed. If Herman Go Home really did stand for HGH — and I was pretty sure it did — Pete Cruz would probably have it in the locker room.

That was the place to go. Even if I had Cruz's medical records, human growth hormone probably wouldn't show up. I remembered reading that urine tests don't really detect HGH and blood tests weren't totally reliable either. That's why it's so hard to prove. But if I caught him in possession of the drug, the truth would come out that Pete Cruz had an unfair advantage over the competition in high school.

I knew Cruz worked out on Wednesdays, so I made sure I lifted on that day. After my workout, I hung around so I would be in the locker room when he was finished. Biding my time until he went to the showers, I prayed he wouldn't lock his locker while he was gone.

I heard the locker door creak, but there was no slam. Yes!

Cruz headed off to the showers — his locker unlocked and half open. From my vantage point to his left, about 15 feet away, I could see some things on the top shelf. But I needed a closer look.

I thought back, Wasn't this the way baseball reporters nailed Mark McGwire with performance-enhancing stuff?

I'd have to move fast. I waited 30 seconds to make sure he was safely in the shower and I could hear the water running. Then I slipped over and poked my nose inside the locker, furiously sorting through the containers. Deodorant, body wash, hair gel — I never knew Pete cared so much about grooming.

Nothing jumped out, until I moved the deodorant and spotted a small plastic container. I nervously glanced behind me and turned the bottle to see the label. Was this it? Was this the damning evidence?

No. It was only aspirin.

I thought I heard the shower shut off, so I closed the locker door to its original position. The sound of footsteps grew ominously louder as I darted back to my own locker. But Pete rounded the corner, draped in a towel, before I got there.

"What the hell are you doing near my locker?!" he bellowed.

"Nothing. I wasn't near your locker," I said, trying to sound convincing. But I could feel sweat running down my face. It wasn't just steam from the shower.

"Yeah you were! If I catch you stealing money, I'll pound you into the ground!"

"I don't steal," I said defensively.

"Then why were ya near my locker?" Cruz demanded to know, raising a menacing fist. The thunderbolt tattoo on his right bicep bulged out like it was going to thrust forward and strike me down.

"I wasn't. I was just leaving."

I grabbed my backpack and shot out of the locker room, not looking back. But I could feel the weight of Pete's icy stare all the way to the door.

So what if I came up empty? He was probably hiding the HGH somewhere else.

CHAPTER 16

"Winners never take a day off! What you do today will make a difference on the field tomorrow," Coach Dawson stressed, after popping his head into the weight room. You could bet he stopped by to take note of every player at the "voluntary" afternoon workout. I made sure he saw me.

A symphony of grunts and groans, augmented by the sound of metal plates crashing down, was the best way to describe the scene that February day as the football team furiously pumped up.

"Ahhhhh!" screamed Greg, as his huge stack of iron shot up to the sky. Meanwhile, Luke Skoronski, our 6-foot-4-inch, 260-pound tackle, straightened his legs and drove 300 pounds of leg press forward like it was merely an afterthought.

But my eyes kept darting over to Cruz, who was still working out with the team, even though he was a senior and wouldn't play another season with us. Between my own lifts, I watched him like a hawk. My interest didn't go unnoticed.

"What's your problem, Jefferson? Quit looking at me, you little maggot," Cruz warned.

"I'm just impressed with how much stronger you've gotten," I responded.

"That's what hard work will do," he shot back. "Try it yourself sometime."

I felt like saying, "What the hell do you think I'm doing, in here three times a week?" but I refrained. However, Greg sprang to my defense.

"Pete, Jason works as hard as anybody here. It's tough coming back from an ACL, but he's gonna make it."

Pete just turned away, acting like he couldn't care less about my challenge.

Greg was definitely assuming a leadership role on the team. He helped younger players with their lifting technique and encouraged everyone around him.

"You're packing some guns!" he remarked to another kid who was a sophomore like me and a backup on last season's team. "You got a license for those?"

The kid smiled as if he'd just been blessed by the Pope.

"Here, let me show you how to use that," he said to another kid. "You need to flex your knees and get your back into it."

Coach Dawson hadn't named the captains for next year's team yet, but it was a safe bet that Greg would be one of them. Still, at least one personality rift remained on the team. Rob Kelley wasn't speaking to Greg, probably still smarting from Greg stealing his girlfriend.

When the workout ended at 4:30, I showered and returned to my locker to get dressed. "They've got to fix those showers," I said to Greg, who was standing in front of his locker, almost dressed. "Half of them don't work. They just dribble."

"I know. I'll say something to Coach about it," he replied.

Greg looked at me with bright eyes as he buttoned his shirt. "Hey Jason, did you hear about next year's schedule?"

"No. What about it?"

"We might be playing a team from Texas. They were talking about it at the banquet."

"You're kidding! Where?"

"We might be playing down *there*, against Plano. They were nationally ranked last year, and we're trying to arrange a game. We both have an open date to fill."

"We might go to Texas?!"

"It's possible, but nothing's for sure yet. We'd have to raise a lot of money to get down there. The Booster Club's working on it."

"Wow, that's what I call a road trip!" I said.

"Yeah, it would be awesome. That would be some game—Illinois vs. Texas! But like I said, it was just being talked about at the banquet. Don't put anything in the *Herald* about it, because it's just in the talking stage."

"Oh, man, I hope we can play them. It would be like a bowl game!" I said.

"Yeah, we could prove ourselves against the best," Greg pointed out.

"So, how was the banquet? Did you get rings?"

Greg reached into his locker, pulled out a large ring with a blue stone in the center, and slid it onto his finger. He held it out for me to admire.

"Who-a-a! Those are nice," I gushed, examining the gold plating and the words "Illinois State Champions."

"That's not all. We also got these," he said, reaching into his gym bag. "I think I have one in here."

After fumbling through the bag for a while, Greg pulled out a T-shirt that must have been buried on the bottom. I immediately noticed that the shirt was in our school colors—blue with gold. He held it up against his broad chest. The bold lettering read: Hillsboro High Eagles, Illinois Class 6-A State Champions.

"Awesome!" I fantasized about wearing that T-shirt and ring.

"Nice, huh?"

"Totally cool! That shirt says it all."

Greg looked at me sympathetically. "I'll get you a shirt," he said without hesitation.

"You can?"

"Sure. You're a part of the team too. It wasn't your fault you got hurt."

I imagined myself wearing that shirt proudly. "Thanks, man! I'd love one!"

"No problem. I can't get you a ring, but I will get you a shirt. You deserve one too."

I reached over and gave Greg a fist bump. "That would be awesome."

"Hey, I gotta go," said Greg, slapping me on the shoulder. "I'm meetin' Marla."

As Greg hurried out of the locker room, I couldn't help but be envious. The guy was not only a state champion, he had the hottest girl in school. Greg had it all.

My eyes drifted down to the ground as I put on my socks. That's when I noticed something on the floor over by where Greg was dressing, maybe something that had fallen out of his locker or gym bag when he reached inside to show me the T-shirt. I walked over to see if it was anything important that needed to be returned.

At first I thought it was garbage, just a small, empty container. It looked like a glass medicine vial. Then I read the label, and a feeling of horror swept over me like an approaching tornado. Glyropin ... HGH.

My God! Could it be Greg?

CHAPTER 17

I rushed home and called Julie.

"Jason! What a nice surprise! What's up?" she greeted, picking up the phone after just two rings.

"You're not going to believe it; I still don't believe it myself. Greg might be doing the HGH," I said in a hushed tone.

"Greg! Your friend? How do you know that?"

"I was talking to him in the locker room today, and when he left I found an empty vial near his locker that said Glyropin. It's a brand name for human growth hormone. It was right on the label."

"Wow! Are you going to ask him about it?" Julie asked.

"I don't know. I don't know if I can do that."

"Well, you can't write a story then," Julie said. "You have to approach him and either get a confirmation or a denial. That's only fair. That's the rule of journalism Mr. McCloud taught us, remember?"

"I remember, but how *can* I write this? Greg's my bud. Let's not jump to conclusions yet."

"You couldn't wait to write the story if Pete Cruz was the one using," she reminded me. "But I understand where you're coming from. This is sticky."

"You know, maybe that vial wasn't Greg's. It could have rolled in front of his locker, or someone may have planted it there to get him in trouble," I suggested. "Who knows? Maybe 'Deep Throat' planted it there to set up Greg. They made a point of telling me to look in the locker room."

"Do you really believe that, Jason?"

"No ...uh, I don't know. I just can't believe it's Greg."

There was a moment of silence on the line. "Wait a minute. Do you remember when he went bonkers on Rob Kelley at the Homecoming dance? Do you think that was because of the HGH? Maybe some kind of 'roid rage?" Julie wondered.

"It could have been," I conceded, after considering the theory. "Greg's usually not like that."

"Drugs change people," she pointed out.

"I know they do. But Greg's solid — a stand-up guy. I can't believe he's taking HGH."

"Well, you got your blockbuster story. But I guess it's true: Be careful what you wish for."

"Do you think I should just drop the investigation?" I asked.

"That's a call you have to make. Just try to be fair and make sure you have all the facts before you write anything."

"I will," I replied. "But Julie, don't breathe a word of this to anyone. Do you swear to that?"

"Of course, Jason. You know you can trust me."

Just because I didn't want Julie to talk didn't mean I couldn't. But only to one person: Frederick. He had to know what I discovered too.

My mind could barely concentrate on school the next day. When I passed Frederick in the hallway between classes, I tried to set up a rendezvous.

"Coach Dawson wants me to meet with him after school to order my supplies. I'm supposed to see him at 4," Frederick said. "Can we meet afterward?"

"Frederick, this can't wait. I've got to talk to you right after school. Can you meet me in the library at 3?"

"Okay. I have to get some things from my locker first, but I'll come right after seventh period."

I was waiting in the library when Frederick strolled in, right on time. "C'mon," I said, grabbing his arm and ushering him over to a secluded corner hidden by bookshelves. "We need as much privacy as we can get."

Ironically, we passed a section on health and fitness books before finding our cove hideaway. I peered around the corner, just to make sure no one was within ear range. But the library was practically deserted.

"Look what I found in the locker room yesterday," I said, silently sliding the empty HGH vial out of my pocket and into Frederick's hand.

Frederick squinted and adjusted his glasses as he examined the container. He stood speechless for a moment, before his eyes darted back up to meet mine.

"Where'd you find this?" he demanded to know.

"In front of a locker."

"Whose?"

I hesitated for a minute. I entered the library fully intend-ing to tell Frederick everything I knew, but now I had sec-ond thoughts. Would he tell Coach Dawson?

Frederick closed his hand around the bottle and scanned the library through a hole in the books. "Whose locker was it?" he repeated.

"Frederick, I don't know how it got there ... but I found it by Greg Maxwell's locker," I said softly.

"Coach has to know about this."

"No!" I protested, grabbing the vial from Frederick's hand. Just then I realized how loud my voice was, so I took it down a notch. "We can't do anything yet. I'm trusting you on this, man. Don't screw me over."

"Then how come you asked me here? You know I have an obligation to report this."

"I'm just asking you to keep things quiet until I gather more evidence. I still don't think it's Greg's. Somebody must have planted it to get him in trouble."

Frederick's face loosened. He looked like he would give me the benefit of the doubt.

"I just need to pick your brain as a trainer, because I know you're smart," I said. He needed some buttering up. I wanted him to feel like we were in this together. "How would this stuff be taken?"

"That's a liquid vial. The contents are injected with a nee-dle, probably shot up into the butt or somewhere with some cushion of fat."

"Shot up? Like a junkie?"

"You might say that."

"And where do you think the person got it?"

"Probably ordered it over the Internet," Frederick said. "This is a dangerous drug without a prescription. Nobody on the team should be taking this!"

"I know, but I'm still investigating. Promise me you won't say anything to Coach Dawson, or anybody else. Can I have your word on that, Frederick?"

I held out my hand to shake. Frederick thought for a second. "I really need to report this," he said.

"No!" My voice sprang out, and I nervously glanced around. "Give me some time to figure this out. I'm trusting you."

I held out my hand again and Frederick grabbed it. He squeezed firmly.

"Okay, but you better keep that bottle hidden," he warned. "If someone catches you with it, they might think you're on HGH."

Frederick left for his meeting with Coach Dawson, and I prayed that I could trust his handshake. I lingered in the library for a few minutes, just so no one would see us leaving together.

"Do you need help finding a book?" offered the librarian.

"Not right now thanks."

Just as I was about to leave, a sweet voice stopped me in my tracks. "Jason, how are you?" I recognized that voice without looking up.

"Good, Sara. How about yourself?"

"Life goes on," she said, giving me a quick hug.

After some idle chatter, Sara steered the conversation to her ex-boyfriend.

"What's going on with Greg? He doesn't talk to me much anymore," she remarked. "Not after the breakup."

"Oh ... uh ... he's fine. I think he'll be named a captain for next season. Maybe."

"That's great. I heard he made all-state."

"Yeah ... he had *some* season."

"Does he ever ask you about me?"

"Sometimes," I said, lying through my teeth. "He still says you're a great girl."

"Then why did he treat me that way," Sara said, lowering her head, her voice trailing off.

"Huh?"

"I don't get it. Why did he change? We'd been together so long."

"What do you mean? How did he change?"

"He just got weird, with a lot of mood swings. He was so unpredictable I didn't recognize him. That's why I had to break up."

"*You* broke up with Greg? I always thought he broke up with you."

"No. I called it off. I didn't want to, but I had to!" Sara said. "Greg isn't right. I think he needs help. Maybe you can figure him out."

"I'm trying," I said. My mind drifted away, and our conversation sputtered to a timeout. *She broke up with him!*

After a moment of dead silence, Sara's voice hastened me back. "Is Greg still thinking about going to Notre Dame?"

"They're recruiting him, along with Michigan, Ohio State, Illinois and a bunch of other schools." No sooner did I say that than I began to think: A scandal could end all that.

"That's so wonderful. I hope he becomes a big college star. I still care about him."

"Sara, let me ask you something. Is Greg afraid of needles?"

"A big guy like Greg? Greg's not afraid of anything — except maybe commitment," she said, rolling her eyes. "I know he's donated blood before. We gave it together last summer at the community center. Needles don't bother him one bit."

"I see," I said, my voice trailing off.

"That's kind of a funny question to ask," Sara said. "Why do you want to know that?"

"Oh, I just wondered ... The guys on the team may have to take a blood test."

"Don't let that worry you, Jason. It only hurts for a second."

"I know. I'm not worried."

"Well, I've got a paper to write," Sara said, "something on the causes of World War II for European history class."

"Good luck with it," I said, before leaving the library.

As I walked out, I wondered if I wanted to be known as the guy who started World War III.

CHAPTER 18

M r. McCloud carefully set up his laptop in the front of the room and projected an image on the white board behind him. Everyone settled into their chairs as the bell rang.

"I want to show you something I discovered online last night," he said, addressing the class. "This blogger broke a national story. The only problem is, he's light on some key facts. Read this and see if you can tell me what they are."

Journalism class fell silent as everyone read the blog. The blogger wrote that some senator from Louisiana was taking kickbacks from a big oil company, money he received to push for more off-shore drilling in the Gulf of Mexico.

"I know. He was vague about the amount of money the senator got. He just wrote 'thousands of dollars,'" someone pointed out after a minute or two.

"And he never even said when the senator took the bribes, or who the oil company was," Julie added.

"Good! Those are pretty gaping holes in the story," Mr. McCloud acknowledged. "What else?"

I raised my hand. "He uses unnamed sources," I answered confidently.

"Bingo! Along with those other serious deficiencies, the story lacks credibility because no one has come out on the record accusing the senator of misconduct, and the evidence is sketchy," McCloud said. "It's just more grist for the rumor mill."

My mind drifted for a second to my own investigation and my unnamed source, 'Deep Throat.'

After some hesitance, I raised my hand again. "Mr. McCloud, what if your source is afraid to reveal their identity for one reason or another? Say ... it will get them in trouble. Aren't you supposed to protect them and not give out their name?"

"Always try to get them to go on the record with their name used, Jason," he replied. "Otherwise, your story may not be taken seriously."

McCloud looked up at the white board and pointed. "This is what passes for journalism these days, and it's garbage," he said with a sigh. "Solid reporting is being replaced by unsubstantiated rumor. Everybody has a blog, and everybody wants to play reporter, but some don't know — or don't follow — the rules. It's amateur hour."

I couldn't afford to turn my investigation into amateur hour. It needed to be done by the book, with no mistakes. Otherwise, no one would take me seriously.

The next day Frederick stopped me in the hallway as fourth period let out. "We need to talk," he said, looking more serious than normal, which, in Frederick's case, was a difficult feat. We ducked into a janitor's closet, which was the only place that came to mind for privacy as the halls began to flood with students. I stepped over a mop and wash bucket and flicked on the light.

"What's up?"

"I think I saw Greg shooting up in the locker room yesterday," Frederick said, without wasting a second.

"What do you mean, you *think* you saw him?"

"I don't know ... I didn't get a real good look. I was pretty far away. But I saw him turn quickly and put something into his gym bag. He had his shorts down at the time."

"When was this? Did anyone else see it?"

"I don't think so. It was late in the day and I was locking up the trainer's room. Nobody else was around."

"Did you actually see a needle, Frederick?"

"I can't be sure. But he definitely had something in his hand."

"What did he say when he saw you looking?"

"Nothing. But he zipped up his bag."

"Did he have any needle marks, from what you saw?"

"I couldn't tell. I don't go around staring at guys' butts."

I began to think back on the blogger in journalism class the day before. Frederick's eyewitness account was shocking but also short on facts. It was like saying you saw Bigfoot, but having no details.

Or maybe I just didn't want to believe him.

"Thanks for telling me," I said. "If you see anything else, let me know."

"Okay. I've got to go," Frederick said. "I'll be late for class."

We opened the door of the janitor's closet and cautiously stepped out. The halls were clearing as the fifth-period bell rang. But a straggler to class spotted us.

"So, what do we have here? You two having a gay relationship in there?" needled Pete Cruz. "Talk about coming out of the closet ..."

What could I say, that we were taking inventory? We hustled off to class before Cruz could tease us some more.

But he got in one more shot. "Frederick, I thought you had better taste than *that*."

For the next few days, I kept thinking about Mr. McCloud's disdain for unnamed sources. Somehow, I needed to find out the identity of my mysterious "Deep Throat" and get him or her on the record, giving up the name of the person on the football team who was doing human growth hormone. I also had to find out *how* they knew. Could they be trusted?

My story lacked teeth without it. As McCloud would say, it was just grist for the rumor mill.

All evidence pointed toward Greg, but maybe he'd be exonerated. I prayed he would be, because I didn't think I could ever write a story that might get my friend in trouble.

Still, I had to know the truth. I guess it was just the journalist in me.

CHAPTER 19

I arranged to meet Julie at Starbucks again. I bought her another caramel latte and we sat down at the same table we had before.

"This is cool, but someday we're going to have to have a night date," she said, fingering her bead necklace. Julie usually wore more jewelry than a pirate, but at least it could all be taken off. She wasn't into piercing her tongue, lips, nose or eyebrows. I hate that look.

I scanned the room, hoping nobody would sit too close to us.

"I like your sweater," she remarked.

"Oh ... thanks," I said, turning my head back to her. "Julie, it's time we learn the identity of 'Deep Throat.' What do you think?"

"Yeah, you need to nail down your source. But how are you going to do that? They obviously don't want their name known."

"I don't know. I have to figure something out."

"I think it's Sara Cooley," Julie opined.

"Sara? You're crazy. She's much too sweet to blow the whistle on Greg."

"You don't know girls," Julie said. "No girl likes to be dumped. What did Shakespeare say? Hell hath no fury like a woman scorned."

"Yeah, but I just talked to Sara a little while ago. And guess what? She broke up with Greg."

"Maybe she's just saying that. Maybe she's one of those psycho chicks who plot revenge? Maybe she carries around a meat cleaver."

"Get serious."

"Well, who do you think 'Deep Throat' is?"

"I don't know, but first we have to look at who would have a motive to turn Greg in. Who would have an ax to grind with him? That's assuming, of course, that it is Greg. I don't know that for sure yet."

"Sara could have a motive," Julie reminded me.

"Let's just forget Sara. I don't think it's her."

Julie and I both sat lost in thought for a moment. "Rob Kelley," she blurted out. "Greg stole his girlfriend, right?"

"Yeah, I'm sure he's still not over losing Marla. Kelley would have a motive —jealousy."

"That makes sense," Julie said, taking another sip of her latte.

Thinking back, I remembered Kelley being in the newsroom the day that the second note appeared. Was that just a coincidence?

"And there's another guy who's jealous of Greg too: Cruz," I pointed out. "He's never liked it that Greg became a bigger star than him."

"You're just saying that because you don't like Pete Cruz. You wanted to pin the HGH on him before, remember? Before you found it near Greg's locker?"

"I'm still not convinced that Cruz is innocent. He's beginning to look like the Incredible Hulk."

Julie drew her head closer to mine and lowered her voice. "Have you ever thought that more than one player could be on HGH? What if the whole team is?"

I considered the theory. "It's possible, I guess. But I have no evidence of that."

"That would *really* be a scandal," Julie said.

"I've got to draw 'Deep Throat' out from hiding. Somehow, I've got to meet him face-to-face. Then I'll know for sure who's doing HGH. The problem is, I don't even know how to contact him."

"Yeah, you have nothing to go on but anonymous notes," Julie acknowledged. "But say 'Deep Throat' does agree to meet with you and he or she is telling the truth. You're still going to have to get them to say something on the record that you can use. The person may be afraid to do that."

"I'll cross that bridge when I come to it," I said. "Right now I have to figure out how to meet 'Deep Throat.'"

Julie gently placed her hand on my arm. "I hope you're prepared for the truth, Jason. It could be ugly."

"I know. All signs point to Greg being dirty," I conceded. "Maybe I'm in denial, but I'm still not totally convinced that he's the user."

I needed to do more research to find out where you'd get HGH online, so I typed in the word "Glyropin" before doing another search under "injectable HGH." The results were frightening.

Glyropin was sold on several sites, and it was pretty affordable. Prices ranged from $18 per bottle to about $60 for a one month supply. Those were discounted prices, according to the sites. But human growth hormone was sold in other forms too—pills, spray, capsules—and some forms were far more expensive.

Some sites said you were required by law to have a doctor's prescription to buy from them, but others offered to sell it without a prescription — no questions asked.

Wasn't there *any* regulation of the drug?

One website displayed a picture of two muscular young people in bathing suits running on the beach. It implied that you, too, could look like them if you injected Glyropin. That same site claimed that their product had no known side effects. It promised faster healing from injuries, loss of body fat, increased muscle size and strength — even increased sexual performance.

But when I searched "injectable HGH" I found another website that told a much different story. It said injecting human growth hormone — using a needle — makes it difficult to achieve optimal levels of HGH in the body. Injections either provide far too high an amount or not enough at all. It recommended taking the drug through a spray mist.

Worst of all, it said injection sites can become infected. I wondered why people would even take it in that form. Maybe price or strength of dose had something to do with it.

All this stuff was scary enough, but then I typed in the phrase "penalties for HGH in Illinois."

In Illinois, it's illegal to possess HGH without a prescription. Distribution of HGH for non-medical reasons is a felony, and someone could get 10 years in prison if they're caught distributing human growth hormone to a person under age 18!

That's when I felt a shiver run down my spine. If Greg was using HGH, I prayed to God he wasn't also giving it to someone else.

CHAPTER 20

"Are you going to eat that last cookie?" Max inquired during lunch.

"No, you can have it," I replied, pushing the oatmeal raisin cookie onto his tray.

"So, what's up with the football team, Scoop?" Kevin remarked.

"Oh, ... uh, nothing," I said. "We've just been lifting weights. Spring practice starts in May."

"I heard we're playing a team from Texas next year. Is that right?" Kevin asked. "Why haven't you written about that?"

"It's not for certain yet."

"Oh yeah? I overheard Coach Dawson talking to someone the other day. He sounded like it was a done deal."

"He did? Maybe I should ask him about it."

"Sure, you could get your byline in the *Herald* again," Kevin said. "I haven't seen it for a while. You need to reach out to your peeps — your loyal readers — again."

Suddenly, a light switch clicked on in my head. "You know Kevin, you're right. A column might be just the way to reach out."

I stopped in Coach Dawson's office the next day we had after-school weightlifting. He smiled and appeared happy to see me.

"Jason, come on in son. I've been meaning to tell you, I'm impressed with how you're working to rehabilitate your knee. I'm anxious to see you run with the ball again in spring practice."

"Thanks, Coach."

"You have a chance to get some playing time next season if your knee's sound. You know we're losing two halfbacks to graduation."

That encouragement was just what I wanted to hear. Once again I felt my interests in a tug-of-war between the football team and reporting.

"What did you come in to see me about?"

"Is it true that we're playing Plano, Texas, next year? I heard people talking about it, but is it finalized yet?"

"We signed an agreement yesterday," Dawson said with a smile. "I talked to their coach over the phone and we worked it out for Sept 22. Our booster club will help pay for the trip, and we're going to hold a fund-raiser. Are you excited?"

"I sure am. That will be great!"

"I think everybody around here is excited," Dawson said. "This will be a wonderful experience for you boys."

"Can I put this in the *Herald* now? Is it okay to print a story saying so?"

"I don't see why not. The only thing standing in the way is the cost of transportation and hotel, and I think we've got that covered."

I pulled out my notepad and interviewed Coach Dawson to get all the details. He suggested I talk to the head of the booster club too. When I walked out of the coach's office, I was sure I had another winning story.

"By the way," Dawson said as I left, "there will be some other news soon too. I haven't announced it yet, but we're going to meet soon to vote on captains."

I called the head of the booster club, Mr. Scinto, to get some quotes. He seemed just as excited about the trip as I was. "It will be a great experience for the players, and it will put Hillsboro High on the football map," Scinto said.

"I'm looking forward to playing down there," I remarked.

"Oh? Are you on the team?"

"Yeah, but I'm a sophomore, and I was out injured last season," I pointed out. I felt a little hurt that he didn't know that.

After the interviews, the only thing that remained was to convince Steven Choi to let me write a column, rather than a news story. In a column, I'd have more freedom to give opinions and write whatever I wanted.

"I know I've never written a column for you, but I've got some great stuff that people will want to read," I said.

"Like what?" he asked.

"Like the team is definitely playing Plano, Texas, next year. We haven't gotten that in print yet."

"That's confirmed?"

"Yeah, I talked to Coach Dawson about it the other day, and I've got all the details."

"Well, why can't you announce it in a straight news story, like hard news? Why do you have to have a column? Dude, we don't give columns to everyone. Especially not sophomores."

"But I'm on the football team, so I can give you real insider information," I pitched. "I know some things going on. In fact, we can call the column 'Inside the Huddle.' "

Steven considered my proposal. "I like the idea," he said, staring off into space. "All right, maybe we can try it. But no picture with the column yet. Some of the older guys, like Dave, might be jealous."

"That's fine. I'll write the story tonight and send it right in to you."

"You'll have to, if you want to make deadline. Our next issue comes out the first week of March," he pointed out.

"Thanks, Steven," I said, giving him a high-five. "Don't worry, it will be good."

That night I worked furiously on the column so I could e-mail it in to Steven.

"Jason, are you doing your homework?" my mom called up from downstairs.

"I'll get to it, Mom. I'm just writing a column for the school paper first."

"See that you do," she said.

I led the column off with the big news, our game in Texas, and tried to write it from a player's perspective while still getting in all the necessary details and quotes. Then I added in some observations from our off-season weightlifting sessions, saying how much bigger and stronger some of the guys were getting. But I didn't imply that human growth hormone might be the reason. I couldn't go there yet. I also wrote that the captains would be selected soon, and predicted that Greg would be a shoo-in.

At the end of the column, I snuck in a secret message.

After school the next day, I found my sports editor in the *Herald* newsroom.

"Did you get my column, Steven? What did you think?"

"I just read it; I've got it on my screen now," he said. "I like it, but I don't get that last paragraph. What's up with this?"

He pointed to the end of my column, where I wrote: 'DT', I need to meet with you badly. Can I get confirmation and talk about the game plan?

"What is this? Does DT stand for defensive tackle or something?"

"Yeah ... uh ... it's just a little closing personal note. Sometimes columnists do that sort of thing," I said. "Please, can we keep it in?"

I held my breath. Steven looked confused. "Other columnists do this, you say?"

"All the time," I assured. I was glad he didn't ask me to name one.

"All right, I'm cool with it, I guess. After all, it's your column."

I silently breathed a sigh of relief, and prayed that my most important reader, 'Deep Throat,' would see the column and figure out the message.

CHAPTER 21

Mid-March arrived and still no word from "Deep Throat." Had he or she read the column? Were they ever going to meet me face to face?

I checked the newsroom mailbox every day. Nothing.

Coach Dawson announced an after-school meeting on March 20 for all returning football players. He wanted us to vote on team captains to have them in place when spring practice rolled around in May.

We crowded into a small section of the locker room that day, the returning starters dominating the available benches while everyone else sat on the floor.

As I scanned the room, I couldn't stop staring at Luke Skoronski, our huge tackle. He looked really weird, really ugly. His jaw and eyebrows jutted out like a caveman. That's one guy who will never be Homecoming King, I thought to myself. But maybe we should elect him captain. When he goes out for the coin toss, he'll scare the hell out of the other team.

"Okay, listen up. I'm going to give each one of you a ballot and you're going to choose three players for captains next year," instructed Coach Dawson. "Give it some thought. Pick the guys that you feel are the best team leaders."

I looked over at Greg and quickly wrote his name down at the top of my ballot. Then I picked an offensive player, Rob Kelley, because the quarterback is always a leader, and I scribbled in Skoronski's name under Kelley, just for kicks.

I folded my ballot and passed it forward, as did the others. We waited for a few minutes while Dawson and one of our assistant coaches stepped away and counted the votes. When they returned, they both looked pleased.

"I'd like to say, I think you made some great choices," Coach Dawson said. "Our tri-captains for next season are Greg Maxwell, Rob Kelley and Marques Caldwell. Let's give them a hand."

As everyone clapped, I wondered how the vote count read. I bet Greg and Rob were close to unanimous picks — but not quite, since I'm sure they didn't vote for each other.

"Congratulations, Greg," I said as the meeting broke up. "I knew you'd be picked."

"Thanks, Jason," he answered, swallowing up my hand with his giant mitt in a firm shake. "The campaigning you did for me in the paper must have helped."

I walked away, wondering if my faith in Greg was justified.

—⬥—

Frederick rushed into the weight room and caught my attention from the doorway, just as I was about to leg press

250 pounds. "I need to talk to you" he signaled, without saying a word. His hand motioned me out the door.

"You can have this, Steve," I said, getting up off the machine.

I followed Frederick out the door and he ushered me down the hallway to a small, deserted room.

"Mike Palumbo just came up to me; he's got some kind of sore near his butt! It could be infected! I sent him to see a doctor," Frederick said, breathlessly.

"Wait a minute. Slow down. Palumbo?"

"Yeah, our defensive end!"

"Why did he come to you?"

"He has this big sore lump and he doesn't feel well. He wanted me to look at it, but I'm not a doctor. I can't treat that!"

"No, of course not. You're a trainer," I said.

"But I do know some things. The lump is red and irritated, and he said it's real painful, with puss and everything. It looked like an abscess. It could be infected. I think he needs antibiotics, which I can't give."

"Do you think he got that from injecting HGH?"

"I saw needle marks in the area," Frederick stated, leaning in closer to me.

I looked Frederick straight in the eye. "Wow! Palumbo is using!"

"What if he's sharing a needle, or re-using a needle. You can get hepatitis B from that! I know that from health class," Frederick pointed out.

"Did you ask him about it?"

"No. I just looked at it and told him to go see a doctor right away. I didn't ask him how he got it, and he didn't say. Maybe I was afraid to ask."

"Did you tell Coach Dawson?"

"Not yet, but I probably should."

"I'm wondering how many players are doing HGH. Have you seen Luke Skoronski lately? He looks like Neanderthal Man!"

"*That* could be a side effect of human growth hormone," Frederick pointed out.

"Frederick, this is getting bigger all the time. Hang with me on this. I'm going to find out the truth."

I returned to the weight room and acted like nothing unusual had happened. I didn't hear anyone talking about Palumbo going home. They probably didn't know about it.

I resumed lifting, but I realized the time had come to confront Greg. I couldn't put it off any longer. What if he was using? And what if he got sick like Palumbo?

I made sure no one was around us in the locker room when I took the big step. It was one of the most difficult conversations I've ever had to start.

"Hi, Greg. How are you feeling?" I probed.

"Great, Jason," he replied, looking over from his locker. "I think I'm in the best shape of my life."

"You've been working hard enough," I noted.

"Gotta get ready for Plano!" he said. "Plus, we need to defend our state championship next year."

"Right. I can't wait for next season," I remarked.

"Hey, I've got something for you," Greg said. He reached into his locker and tossed me the championship T-shirt he promised. "It's a large; it should fit."

"Oh, thanks! I really appreciate this," I said, holding up the shirt to admire it.

"How's your knee doing? You're looking stronger."

"Yeah, it feels fine now."

"Good, because you're going to be an important part of the offense next season. I just know it," Greg said with a smile.

This was getting harder by the minute. I felt the urge to just walk out and forget about questioning him, but this was my chance. I summoned my courage.

"Greg, I need to ask you about something."

"Shoot."

I swallowed hard. "I found an empty container in the locker room last month that said Glyropin-HGH on the label. It's a performance-enhancing drug. Do you think any of our players could be using it?"

Greg stood silent for a few seconds. The awkward pause made me uncomfortable. Did he hear what I said? Would he even answer me?

Finally, Greg turned his head to me, looking expressionless. "What makes you think that? Where'd you find it anyway?"

I gulped hard and spit out the truth. "Right around here," I said, motioning to the floor around his locker.

Greg slammed his locker shut. "Is that right? Well, I sure don't know anything about it."

"You don't know anybody who's using HGH?"

"Sure don't."

"Okay, I just thought I'd ask," I said, not willing to push any further. "That stuff can really mess up your health. No one should be using it."

Greg nodded, without saying another word.

Two days later, the fateful note appeared in my mail slot. I snatched the envelope and ripped it open.

Meet me next Thursday at 4 p.m. in the home dugout on the school baseball field.

I couldn't believe my eyes! The mystery was about to be solved. I was finally going to meet "Deep Throat." Not in a dark, mysterious parking garage — like Bob Woodward's clandestine rendezvous with his source in "All the President's Men" — but on a frozen baseball field.

I braced myself for the truth. As Julie said, it could be ugly.

CHAPTER 22

I sat alone in the baseball dugout, my ears searching for a voice—no matter how distant—my eyes straining for a silhouette to emerge on the horizon. "Deep Throat," my mysterious source for the entire four-month investigation, was about to be revealed on a blustery, gray March afternoon.

I checked the time on my cell phone. The note said to meet at 4 p.m., and it was now 4:05. *Don't blow me off!*

The snow on the pitcher's mound had nearly melted away, leaving a muddy mess. My story was a muddy mess, too, unless I could confirm my explosive information. I had to meet my Deep Throat face to face.

This wasn't some puffy high school feature I was writing. It was hard news! It could result in jail time, for God's sake!

Where is he—or she?

Suddenly I heard footsteps ... and a shadow crept forward from behind the dugout.

The figure was bundled in a hooded ski jacket and snow boots. I wasn't immediately able to see the face, hidden behind large sunglasses. Then the hood pulled back and blonde hair spilled out.

Marla!

"Marla! You're Deep Throat?!"

She nodded without saying a word.

"You've been sending the notes? Why couldn't you talk to me?"

Marla's beautiful face looked etched with pain. "Because it's Greg. Greg's doing HGH," she said sadly.

"Oh my God, I was afraid of that," I said. "Look what I found near his locker." I pulled out the Glyropin-HGH vial.

Marla reached into her ski jacket and handed me a similar-looking bottle. "Here's another one," she said ruefully. "He's ordering it over the Internet. I checked the history on his computer and found out."

"I knew it was probably Greg, but I never wanted to believe it. I don't know what to do about this now," I said.

"Have you talked to Greg about it?" she asked. "You're his friend."

"I tried to, but he denies it."

"He won't talk about it with me either, but he knows I know. I keep telling him it could kill him, but all he says is, 'This will make me a better player.' He thinks he needs it to play at Notre Dame."

"That's crazy," I shot back. "Greg's a great player without drugs."

"I know, but try telling him that!"

"Marla, why couldn't you just come out and tell me about Greg's problem. All those notes were like a puzzle I had to solve. Herman Go Home?"

"I wanted you to figure it out yourself. I don't want to be linked to this in any way. Greg can't know I came to you."

"But what do you want me to do? I've already talked to him, and he won't tell me a thing."

"Write something," she said forcefully. "We can't let this go any further. That drug will destroy him."

"I always wanted to break the story, but that was before I knew for sure it was Greg. I don't know if I can do it now."

"You have to!" Marla shot back, her voice bordering on hysterical. "For Greg's sake and the sake of the other players!"

"Others? Is Greg giving HGH to other players?"

Marla just nodded, looking down at the frozen ground.

"So that's how Palumbo and Skoronski got it. Is anybody else using?"

"I don't know. I don't know how many are involved," she said, shaking her head.

"How long has Greg been using HGH?"

"It started during the season. That's all I know." Marla was looking more desperate by the minute.

"You've got to expose this — right now. Write an article for the paper. That's the only thing that will stop it. Greg can't go on like this!"

"But Marla, if I write a story I'll need to include the evidence. And I'll need to use you as a source on the record."

I started to pull out my tape recorder from inside my coat. Marla looked terrified at the sight of it, like I was holding a tarantula.

"No! I can't do that!" she protested. "Greg can't know I'm involved! You have to keep my name out of the story. Say you're protecting your source."

"Okay, I'll try to," I assured, stuffing the recorder back in my pocket. "But I still don't know if I can even bring myself to write something."

"You have to! I love Greg. I can't watch him destroy himself like this, and look what he did to me." She yanked off her sunglasses, revealing a badly swollen black eye. "I haven't been in school for two days."

I felt my stomach drop. "Greg gave you that?!"

"Just the other night. He flew into a rage. And that's not all."

Marla pushed up her coat sleeve and unveiled a massive bruise on her arm. It was turning yellow.

"Believe me, it used to be a lot darker. I've had it for about a week."

"Oh, Marla ... I can't believe he did that to you."

"I even threatened to break up with him if he didn't get off the stuff," she revealed.

Then Marla hit me with one last line that haunted me through restless nights: "Do it for Greg, and do it for the team."

"I've got to go now. Give me a head start so nobody sees us together," Marla said, before slipping off into the gathering late-afternoon darkness.

I sat alone in the dugout for a while, just to think. There was no use pretending, no denying it anymore. My heart sunk with the final realization: Greg was in *big* trouble.

That night I called Julie and told her the news.

"Deep Throat is Marla?" she burst out into the phone. "You're kidding me? I never would have guessed that!"

"Yeah, I was pretty shocked too. When they said meet at the baseball field, I thought for sure it was a guy."

"And what did she say?"

"She said Greg's doing HGH — and some other players too. We don't know how many."

There was an awkward silence at the other end of the phone. "Julie, are you still there?"

"I'm here. I'm just trying to wrap my head around this. You've got a major story here ... I mean a MAJOR story."

"I know. But can I write it?"

"You have to. You've been chasing this story for months now and people's health is at stake. You're the one who wanted to do hard news, now you've uncovered the biggest story the *Herald*'s ever seen."

"Yeah, Marla told me the same thing: Do it for Greg, and do it for the team. But I also need to do it for her. I think Greg may have hit Marla. She has a nasty black eye."

"So that's why I haven't seen her in school ... Wow, it must really be bad if she wants you to write something that turns in her boyfriend."

"I don't think she realizes that Greg could get jail time for this," I quickly pointed out. "This is serious stuff."

"I know it is. That's why you have a responsibility to act. For Marla's sake. And, somebody's going to get really sick if you don't."

"Somebody already has," I muttered, but I don't think she heard me.

"Why are you hesitating? You have the evidence — a bottle ..."

"I've got two bottles," I interrupted. "Marla gave me one too."

"Then she's really on your side! You've got her as your main source."

"Not so fast," I said. "She doesn't want me to use her name. She wants the story written, but she wants to stay out of it."

"Then just call her an unnamed source."

Now, the silence came from my end of the telephone.

"Hel . . . . . lo? What's the problem?"

"This isn't that easy," I pointed out. "If I write this, I'm also sabotaging my own chances to play next year. Do you think Dawson will play me after I turn in some of my teammates? He'll hate me for it."

"If he cares about his players he won't hold it against you, he'll thank you."

"But I'm also throwing dirt on last year's team. If they were using performance-enhancing drugs during the season, they cheated to win the state championship."

"That's right. It wasn't fair."

"There's also Greg," I said somberly. "How can I turn in a friend? He could get locked up for this, especially if he sold it."

"Maybe it won't come to that," Julie said. "I sure hope it doesn't."

"Oh, girls don't know anything about loyalty. You guys are used to back-stabbing."

"No we're not!" Julie objected.

"Loyalty means everything to me, because I never had it growing up."

"What do you mean?

"I just never got it ... that's all."

"From friends?" Julie wondered.

"No, it goes deeper than that." Suddenly, I was about to pour out a family secret I had always kept quiet. In a moment of high emotion, I felt unusually comfortable spilling my guts to Julie, the hippie chick with a disarming personality.

"You know I live with my mother, right?"

"Yeah, I figured your parents were divorced. Aren't they?"

"Well, they're not quite divorced."

"Where's your dad then?"

"My father skipped out on us when I was seven. He just left home one day and never came back."

There was a moment of silence on the other end of the phone. "Oh, Jason, I'm so sorry. That's awful! Do you ever hear from him?"

"Not a word. For all I know, he could be dead."

"That really sucks!" Julie said, her voice turning angry.

"I kept praying he'd come back, but it never happened. I think he might have run off with another woman. Finally, I just gave up hope, and so did my mom. She had a long talk with me about loyalty and commitment — the importance of never abandoning someone."

"And you feel you're not being loyal to Greg? I understand."

"He's my friend, isn't he? Greg set me straight when I was growing up, like a big brother would. He was there for me."

"Which is the reason you need to help him," Julie quickly replied. "If a story is the only way to get him off HGH, you need to write it."

"I don't know; I don't want to get him in trouble."

"He'll be in more trouble if you don't write it."

Julie was extremely convincing. But before I could even conceive of writing a story that would surely explode through the hallways of Hillsboro High, I had to reach out to Greg one more time.

CHAPTER 23

I caught up to Greg two days later. I'd seen him in passing before that, and even in weight training, but never in a situation where we could talk. I needed to have him alone.

The only time I found him away from Marla or the football team was during seventh-period study hall. He asked Mrs. Baker if he could go to the bathroom. When I saw that, I asked her too, about a minute later.

I swung the boys' room door open, but no one was in there. Where was Greg?

I looked all around. The bathroom was quiet, but when I crouched down I spotted two legs behind the door of one of the toilet stalls.

Stalling for time, I stepped up to the urinal and unzipped my fly, even though I didn't have to go. I wasn't leaving until Greg came out.

A slight groan came from the stall, and I heard the toilet paper roll move. But I never heard the toilet flush. Then I heard the door lock slide open, and Greg emerged.

I looked straight ahead over the urinal, staring at some graffiti that read, "for a good time, call 312-544-8730 ..." I didn't want Greg to see me looking over at him coming out of the stall. I didn't even acknowledge him for a few seconds, and I tried to act surprised.

"Greg! What's up?"

Greg looked startled to see me, and really flustered.

"Jason! Wh-a-a-a-t are you doing here?"

How do you answer a stupid question like that? "Just had to go," I replied.

Greg had some kind of small plastic case in his right hand. But he quickly stuffed it in his pocket before I could get a good look.

He turned quickly and headed for the door.

"Wait!" I called out. "I need to talk to you." I zipped up my fly and took a few steps toward him.

"I gotta get back to study hall," Greg insisted.

There was no time to beat around the bush. "Greg, we've been friends a long time," I reminded him, trying to quickly break the ice. "You know I've got your back. But I have to ask you something again: Are you taking human growth hormone?"

"I told you before, I don't know anything about it," he shot back. "What? Did you follow me into the bathroom to spy on me?"

"Well, what were you doing in the stall? I didn't hear the toilet flush."

"That's none of your business!"

"Greg, I've got pretty good information that you are doing HGH. Please, you've got to stop!"

"Get the hell out of my life!" Greg exploded, charging at me with rhinoceros speed. I stood in shock and quickly tried to brace myself as he shoved me backward. My head banged into the paper towel dispenser, and I crumpled to the ground.

Greg stormed out of the bathroom, not saying a word.

I slowly picked myself up off the floor, still stunned. This was Greg, the old friend who gently carried me off the playing field when I tore my ACL, the guy I'd known all my life. He just went after me like a crazed pit bull!

So this is what HGH does to people? Now I knew what Marla must have put up with. The guy people affectionately called The Barbarian had actually become one!

My head throbbed. As I struggled back to study hall, I felt a lump on the back of my head. But I didn't want to make a big deal about it by going to the nurse's office, so I quickly sat back down in class and avoided eye contact with Greg. I couldn't believe he attacked me like that.

When the seventh-period bell mercifully rang, I was the first one out of class, rushing down to Mr. McCloud's room to see if Gina was in the newsroom. She wasn't there yet, so I sat and waited, trying to wrap my head around — as Julie would say — the bathroom incident. Greg was out of control. He needed help — immediately.

Melissa Franklin, a copy editor at the *Herald*, walked in soon after me.

"Where's Mr. McCloud?" she asked.

"I don't know. I'm just waiting here to see Gina," I replied.

"She's not coming in today. I just saw her take the bus home."

"Great," I muttered, kicking a desk with my sneaker. "The one day she's not here ... Well, if you see her tomorrow, tell her I have to talk to her."

"Hey, what happened to your head?" Melissa asked as I turned to walk out. "You're bleeding back there."

"It's nothing," I answered, continuing on my way. I stopped at my locker and threw on my Cubs hat to conceal the cut.

I could have brought my story to the sports editor, Steven, but I didn't think he had the authority to okay a story this big for the paper. He would have just brought it to Gina for her approval. Why waste time? I might as well go straight to Gina.

That night, I kept thinking about the incident, even when I went to bed. My resolve to break the story only grew stronger—not because I was mad at Greg, but because I needed to help him.

Finally, the next day, Gina and I did hook up in the newsroom.

"What do you want me for, Jefferson?"

"C'mon, let's go outside for a minute. We need to talk without anyone around."

"About what? It's cold out there."

"I'll tell you when we get outside."

"Can't we talk indoors?"

"No. Just come with me. This is really important."

"All right, but I have to get my coat. Make it fast; I've got work to do."

We stepped out a side door into a blustery, overcast day. It was March 30, but winter's chill still clung to the early spring air.

"All right, Jefferson, what's so secret?" Gina asked.

"I've been investigating the football team for months now and I've found some of the players are using HGH. It's a performance-enhancing drug that's illegal without a prescription."

Gina's ears perked up. "What? How do you know this?"

"I have sources, and I found an empty vial of HGH in the locker room."

"Can you trust your sources?"

"Completely. I know for sure who one of the players is, and there are others I'm almost certain about too."

"Will these sources give their names and identify the users in a story?"

"One might," I said, thinking of Frederick. "But the other doesn't want their name used, and I swore I'd protect their identity."

"I'll have to run it by Mr. McCloud first," Gina said. "And you know how he feels about unnamed sources. I don't think he'll go for it."

"Then we have to go around McCloud," I demanded. "This is too big a story to sit on."

"That's easy for you to say. I have to watch what we publish," Gina said. "With something like this, we could be sued."

Gina was being really obstinate. Still, she seemed intrigued.

"Name me the players who you think are using drugs."

"Greg Maxwell, Dave Palumbo and Luke Skoronski," I rattled off. "And I've got proof."

"You've got unnamed sources, and you haven't actually seen those players taking drugs, have you?"

"What do I have to do, show you the needle marks on their butts?!" I shot back.

"No, I'd rather not see that," Gina said, raising her hands up like a shield.

"Why do you think Palumbo was out of school for a while? And why do you think Skoronski's face looks so weird these days? They're on HGH!"

"Maybe they are," Gina acknowledged. "But you still need to pin down your sources or we can't print it. I'm going back inside."

I left too, to go down to the gym to see if Frederick was around. I still hadn't told him about my meeting with 'Deep Throat.'

I also wanted to make sure Frederick would speak on the record if I needed him to do so. His testimony about Palumbo's sickness and the needle marks was crucial. Plus, I already had one unnamed source in Marla. I couldn't afford another one.

I caught up with him just as he was about to leave. "I'll do it," he said, without hesitation. "This whole thing has to stop."

Armed with that commitment, I rushed back to the *Herald* newsroom and Gina. Mr. McCloud was about to close up his room, which was fine with me because it forced Gina outside into the hallway, where I could give her another sales pitch.

"One of my sources says he'll definitely speak on the record," I pointed out. "Can we go with it?"

"Is it your main source?"

"No, it's not," I said reluctantly.

"Then we can't go with it," Gina said dismissively.

Just then Mr. McCloud closed his door and stuck the key in the lock. "Gina, how's the next issue coming?"

I glared at her hoping she wouldn't say anything about my story.

"I'm kind of short on copy right now," she said, "and I don't have any real exciting stories."

"Well, we'll have to try to find some," McCloud said. "This is our fifth issue, the last of the year. We want to make it a good one."

I made eye contact with Gina again, giving her an exasperated look that said, "You know I can fix that."

"Do you two have rides home?" McCloud wondered. We both said yes.

"Then I'll see you tomorrow," he said, striding down the empty hallway.

"Gina, I swear my story is accurate," I said, as soon as McCloud was out of hearing range. "Give it a chance."

"Why should I? I was burned by you before, Jefferson. Remember the Pete Cruz story? He said some things off the record but you printed them."

"I don't even want to talk about that. I handled that story right, and it was one of the best features we ran all year."

Gina zipped up her coat and was about to head off. I grabbed her backpack and handed it to her.

"Just think some more about my investigative story," I urged. "If it runs, people will never forget you as editor of the *Hillsboro Herald*."

CHAPTER 24

Time was running out. Somehow, I had to convince Gina to run my story in the upcoming issue of the *Herald* or it would never see the light of day.

I asked Mr. McCloud again if we were putting out just one more issue of the *Herald*.

"That's right, Jason. The May issue is our last," he confirmed. "If you have a story, you better get it in by April 10."

That gave me just four more days. I needed some advice. How was I going to break down Gina?

Again, I turned to Julie.

"Write it first and show her what you have," she suggested. "If you write a good story and include all your facts, she'll have to run it."

"But what about Marla? I can't use her name or it would be like betrayal. She trusts me."

"Then don't use it. If you write a strong story, you may not need her name. But you need to keep pushing. You can't wait until next year. This has to get out now."

"Yeah, I know. If we wait 'til next season, the whole team might be hooked on human growth hormone."

I spent the next two nights writing and rewriting my story, painstakingly working to make it sound as professional as possible. Even though I danced around identifying my primary source, I felt the story held up. I printed it out and showed a copy to Julie.

"Change this," she pointed out. "Don't say 'butt.' Posterior region sounds better, or even gluteus maximus. And I wouldn't say 'the benefits of HGH are ...' I'd say 'the purported benefits of HGH are ...' Otherwise, your story is awesome!"

"Thanks Julie."

"I see you don't give the players' names. Do you think you should?"

"I gave that a lot of thought," I said. "I kept going back and forth. Finally, I decided not to."

"Well, the story is still powerful. Show it to Gina. And hurry!"

Less than two days remained before the *Herald* deadline. I went to pay one last visit to Gina after school in the newsroom.

"She's out sick today," someone said.

My heart sunk like the Titanic. How could Gina be out sick, this close to deadline? I had to see her!

I almost gave up hope. But that night, I continued to tinker with the story.

Luckily, Gina showed up for school the next day, on Friday.

"Jefferson, I feel like crap and I'm totally stressed out. I've got to get this paper out today and make it read decent," she squawked when I rushed up to her after school in the newsroom.

"I can help you," I said. "Just give me five minutes."

"Is this about that story of yours again?"

"I want you to read it. Five minutes is all I ask. C'mon, let's step outside."

"I'm not going outside the building again. That's probably how I got sick."

"Okay, just in the hallway then."

Gina and I stepped outside and I pulled her into an empty room. "Just please read it," I begged, handing her a copy of the first page.

By Jason Jefferson

Human growth hormone, a dangerous performance-enhancing drug, has been found in the Hillsboro High football team's locker room. This reporter has learned that at least three players on the team, including a tri-captain, have been using the drug, commonly referred to as HGH.

HGH, which is illegal to possess in the state of Illinois without a prescription, can lead to increased risk of heart disease, cancer, bone muscle disease and diabetes, if abused. Its purported benefits include muscle growth and growth in weight and height, giving players a competitive advantage.

The team tri-captain has been found in possession of two empty vials of Glyropin, a brand name for an HGH product.

"I think he's been using it since the middle of last football season," said an unnamed source who is close to the situation.

The source said the HGH product was obtained over the Internet.

Another source, football team student trainer Frederick Hall, confirmed that he has treated a player with needle marks in his posterior region. The drug is commonly injected with a needle.

The investigation comes on the heels of a dream season in which the Eagles captured the Class 6-A state title and were ranked No. 1 in Illinois.

"What do you think? We need to run this," I pleaded to Gina.

"This is a hot story, all right," she conceded. "But I'm still worried about the unnamed source. Mr. McCloud hates those."

"Then do an end run. Go around him," I said.

Gina seemed to at least be considering my plea. I jumped on offense again, trying to break her down with my two-minute drill.

"If we run this it's like doing a public-service story. We could be saving lives," I pointed out.

Times were desperate. All options were on the table. I shifted into my strategy of appealing to her super-sized ego.

"This is your last issue as editor-in-chief. Don't you want to go out with a bang? This story will make you famous. It'll launch your journalism career."

I continued in attack mode.

"You said yourself you don't have any great copy for the May issue," I reminded her. "This is that breakout story you're looking for!"

I could see Gina was thinking long and hard. I held my breath, anxiously awaiting an answer as she stared down at the copy.

Finally, her face lightened. "What the hell, I'm graduating in two months anyway. I'm probably crazy, but I'm going to take a leap of faith on this, Jason. I'll sneak it in."

I let out a huge sigh of relief. "Thanks, Gina! You won't regret it."

"This is hard news. We're going to run it out front. But I'm going to change the lede where you say 'This reporter has learned ...' and make it 'The *Herald* has learned ...' This is the *Herald*'s investigation, not yours."

I was bothered by that change. After all, how much did the paper have to do with getting the story? I did all the legwork on my own. But for the sake of getting it in print, I readily agreed.

"Give me the rest of your story," Gina said, and I handed her page two. "Don't say anything to anybody about this. I'll pull a photo, and create a hole on page one."

At that moment, I could have kissed her.

CHAPTER 25

When May 1st rolled around, I got the mayday distress call.

"Jason Jefferson and Gina Giantoli, please report to the principal's office immediately!"

The paper had just been delivered to school less than an hour ago, but already everyone was buzzing about the story headlined: **Football team in drug scandal**. The story was also uploaded onto the *Herald*'s website.

The P.A. announcement caused quite a stir in my 1 o'clock science class.

"O-h-h-h, you're in trouble now."

"Go get 'em Jason!"

"Don't back down, man."

Feeling proud but a little scared, I picked up a hallway pass and departed class.

"Dead man walking!" someone shouted out, and all I could hear was laughter behind me.

Just outside the main office, I ran into Gina.

"I knew this was coming," she said, looking fearful.

"Stay strong Gina. We're right on this," I assured her.

We walked into Principal Healey's office and immediately spotted Mr. McCloud sitting there. He didn't look happy. His mustache was curled tightly.

"Sit down Gina and Jason," Principal Healey said, looking grave. He had a copy of the *Herald* in his hand.

"This article on the football team that appeared in the *Herald* today, it's my understanding that Mr. McCloud never saw it before it went to print?"

"No he didn't," Gina admitted.

"Why not? This story is extremely inflammatory."

"I know, but it's all true," I spoke up. "I have proof."

Mr. McCloud jumped in. "I don't know if it is or not, but that's beside the point. You know all stories have to pass by me first. Why didn't I see this? You changed the layout I approved."

"We were afraid you'd kill it," I said.

"I'm troubled about the content, but I'm also troubled about the blatant disregard for school procedure," Healey scolded. "Mr. McCloud is the newspaper's adviser. For you to circumvent his authority is just unconscionable."

"I'm especially disappointed in you, Gina," McCloud said, looking at her coldly.

"The story came in right at deadline," she said, trying her best to mount a credible defense. "It was late-breaking and it was really important."

"This story is all true," I chimed in. "It had to get out."

"Don't you think Mr. McCloud should have been the one to decide that?" Healey bellowed. "Students don't make that call. My phone will be ringing off the hook tomorrow, once parents see this." He shook the paper at me to underscore his point.

"It should be! This is serious stuff," I pointed out. I was amazed how brazenly defiant I sounded.

"I can assure you that we will investigate this matter," Healey said. "If your information is accurate, appropriate steps will be taken with the police. What I want you to do now is tell me everything you know about this alleged drug use on the football team. I'm going to speak to Coach Dawson about this too."

I proceeded to rehash my investigation for McCloud and Healey, starting from the beginning when I received my first anonymous tip back in November. I gave a thorough account of everything — my research into performance-enhancing drugs, my observations, the names of the suspected offenders and my sources, except for one. I didn't give up Marla's name.

"You've certainly pursued this aggressively," Healey said, looking slightly impressed. "Why won't you tell us who turned Greg Maxwell in?"

"I'm protecting my source," I answered.

McCloud cracked a slight smile for the first time. "I guess he got that from the movie I showed in class, 'All the President's Men' " he said, turning to the principal.

"That's what Bob Woodward would have done," I noted.

Healey showed a trace of a smile too, looking over at McCloud. Then he abruptly turned stern again.

"You paint a disturbing picture here, Jason. I want you to bring in the HGH containers you have and I'll turn them over to the police tomorrow. They're going to look into this, and they'll probably want to interview you. In the meantime, I'm going to speak to the three players you named. Is there anything else you want to tell us?"

Gina, who sat there silently for most of the hour we were trapped in the office, said no. I threw out one last request.

"Greg Maxwell is my friend," I said. "I wrote this story to save him. I hope the police will be fair with him."

"I'm sure they will be," Principal Healey said. "Now you two head to your seventh-period classes. Mrs. Polansky will write you a pass."

Gina let out a sigh of relief as we left the office and entered the hallway. "That was rough, but you did a good job defending the story, Jason."

For the first time all year I felt close to Gina. She was actually on my side for a change. We were in this together, and we weren't backing down.

On May 2 Frederick and I were individually interrogated by the Hillsboro Police in the school offices. I revealed everything I knew, just like I had to Principal Healey, and turned over the empty Glyropin-HGH vials — the one I found and the one Marla gave me.

In the interview, I told Detective Monson what Marla had told me: Greg was buying the drugs online and you could find the website on his computer history. Only, I still referred to Marla as "my main source."

"I want to talk to your source," said Det. Monson, a thin, wiry man with a dark mustache.

I thought hard. This was the police asking now. It was kind of intimidating. Still, I felt I had the right to protect Marla's identity. I refused to give her name.

"I can't give up the name, because the person is close to Greg and spoke on the condition of anonymity," I said.

Det. Monson looked a little angry as he leaned in on me. He probably expected me to just cave and hand over my source's name.

"You won't cooperate with me on this? You're acting just like a real reporter."

"I consider myself a real reporter," I asserted.

"This investigation will go much smoother if I can speak with your main source, your 'Deep Throat,' as you've called him or her," he said.

I stuck to my principles. "I can't give you the name. The person trusts me."

"I may need to have it," he stressed. "But for now, we'll proceed without it."

"What are you going to do next?"

"I'm going to obtain a search warrant for the Maxwell house," Det. Monson revealed.

"What do you think you'll find?"

"We'll seize his computer and check the hard drive, and we'll search the house for illegal drugs. If we find he's trafficked the Internet for HGH, we'll likely notify the DEA about the website. Unfortunately, a lot of these websites that market human growth hormone operate outside the United States, in places like China. They're difficult to crack down on."

"So, Greg and the other guys haven't admitted to anything yet?"

"No. I met with your principal earlier this morning. They're sticking with their stories. They all deny using HGH."

"That's not true!" I said.

"We'll find out if it's true or not," he said, getting up to leave. "Thanks for your testimony."

Testimony — the word sounded so harsh, like I was ratting out someone in court. I felt conflicting feelings start to seep back into my soul. Was I doing the right thing, or was I just trying to make a name for myself as a journalist? Would everything end up all right for Greg and the others? By sounding the alarm, was I really helping them?

I wanted to reach out to Marla for comfort, but I was sure she was terrified to be seen with me. Half of the school was cool with my story, but the other half acted like I was a traitor.

I skipped weight-lifting practice the next afternoon. I couldn't face my teammates or Coach Dawson. Instead, I hung out in the main office after school with Frederick. We talked to Principal Healey some more, and he asked us more questions.

"Have you heard anything from the police?" I asked. "They said they were getting a search warrant."

"Nothing yet, Jason."

"Are they searching the Palumbo and Skoronski houses too?" Frederick wondered.

"I don't know. That's police business."

Just then the principal's phone rang. He picked up and listened patiently to the caller. But I could tell by the way he held the phone three inches from his ear that the caller was upset.

"Yes ma'am, we're trying to get to the bottom of this. The police are investigating," Healey spoke into the phone. "We'll know more soon."

No sooner did Healey hang up than another call came through.

"No sir, we still haven't cancelled plans for the Texas trip. That game's still on for now," Healey stated. He slammed the phone down.

"It's been crazy around here the last two days. From the number of phone calls I'm getting, I'd say a lot of parents have read your story," he said to me. "We've got a possible drug scandal on our hands and that last parent is more concerned that his son won't get to go to Texas! There's something wrong with that."

Frederick and I looked at each other at the same time. He was probably wondering who the parent was too.

Just then Det. Monson barged into the principal's office with Mrs. Polansky a step behind.

"Mr. Healey, I've got a warrant for the arrest of Greg Maxwell. Is he still in school?"

I gasped when I heard those cold, hard words.

"What are the charges?" Healey asked.

"Possession and distribution of an illegal substance to persons under 18 years of age. We're taking him in for questioning."

"I see. Do you have evidence?" Healey asked.

"We have sufficient evidence to warrant an arrest and further interrogation," Monson replied.

Principal Healey looked at me and Frederick. "Is Greg with the football team now?"

"Yes, they're lifting weights from about 4 o'clock to 5,"

Frederick volunteered.

"Okay, I'll take you to him," Healey said. He and Det. Monson immediately left for the gym, while Frederick and I lingered by the front of the school. Neither one of us wanted to be present at the actual arrest.

I peered into the trophy case that greeted visitors to Hillsboro High, the Illinois state championship trophy proudly displayed up front.

"Did you ever think the season would end like this?" I remarked.

"Never," Frederick said. "That trophy has sure lost its luster."

Word traveled fast. A crowd of students began to gather outside at the front of the building where the squad car was parked. We stepped outside and saw Greg being led back to the police car in handcuffs.

"Detective, are the handcuffs really necessary?" Healey asked.

"It's standard procedure," Monson replied.

I could see Greg look over at the rapidly growing crowd as he was escorted to the police car. His dead eyes met mine, but he didn't say anything. He just looked sad.

Det. Monson opened the back door of the car and led Greg in, pushing Greg's head down so he wouldn't hit it on the roof. A hard metal screen separated the front seat from the back. Greg looked like he was caged.

Some in the crowd booed as Greg was led away, but most stood silent, taking in the bizarre scene.

The police car's back door slammed shut with jarring finality. As the car slowly rolled away, the crowd began to disperse. I turned to head back toward the school and spotted a familiar face standing by a wall in the far back. I knew she didn't want to be seen with me, so I waited for the crowd to go before approaching her.

Marla was in tears.

"I'm sorry," I said. "I hope Greg will be okay."

"That was hard to watch," Marla said, wiping her eyes with her sleeve. "Real hard."

"You think Greg will be sent to jail?"

Marla looked like she was collecting herself. Surprisingly, she seemed calmer, even though I brought up the frightening word "jail."

"Greg is 17," she pointed out. "My uncle is a cop in Milwaukee and I talked to him awhile back. He said Greg would be considered a youthful offender and won't serve jail time. He may have to enter a drug rehab program for counseling, but his record will be cleared if he stays out of trouble. This should be his wake-up call."

I felt the lingering anxiety purge from my body. Greg was right when he said there was a lot more to Marla than people knew. She not only had foxy good looks, she was as sly as a fox too.

"If we had waited much longer, Greg would be 18 and a senior. Then it could have been *real* bad," Marla explained.

"Thank you for reaching out to me on this," I said.

"Well, it got to the point where I had to meet with you. Greg's mood swings were terrible. He wasn't the same guy."

"Yeah, I know. I saw that too — believe me," I said, feeling the back of my head.

"Thank you for keeping my name out of the story," Marla said. "I don't want Greg to ever know I was involved."

"Don't worry. For all he knows, Pete Cruz may have been 'Deep Throat.' "

By this time there was no one else around. Marla gave me a warm hug. It felt special coming from the best-looking girl in school, and one of the most caring.

"Just one thing I've been wondering about," I said before she left. "You called yourself 'Deep Throat' in the messages. How do you even know about 'All the President's Men'?"

"I took journalism two years ago," she said with a wink. "I watched the movie in class, and I read the book. I loved it too."

CHAPTER 26

The results of the police investigation came out a day later. Four Hillsboro High football players were charged with possession of human growth hormone without a prescription: Greg Maxwell, Mike Palumbo, Luke Skoronski and defensive tackle Vernon James. In addition, Greg was charged with distributing the drug to minors. Apparently, everyone got their Glyropin from him.

Vernon James? The scandal was bigger than I thought, but at least it didn't involve the entire team.

The players were all released on bond with a promise to appear in court. They were soon back in school, keeping a low profile.

Pete Cruz was not named. I guess my suspicion of him was wrong after all. He really had gotten bigger naturally.

I called Det. Monson to find out more. It wasn't for the newspaper anymore. That ship had sailed; there were no more issues. I just needed to know if Marla was right about the penalties.

"Under further police interrogation, they all confessed," Monson said. "Maxwell admitted to selling the drug to the others."

"Greg confessed to that?"

"Yes, after we executed the search warrant."

"What's going to happen to them now?" I asked. "Will they go to jail?"

"That's for a judge to decide, but I don't think it will come to that," Monson said. "They're all juvenile offenders, so the charges will probably be dismissed after court-ordered counseling and probation. If they stay clean, they'll be okay. And I think they will. They were all pretty remorseful."

I breathed a sigh of relief. Marla was right.

"That's good. We need them back on the football team," I noted.

"You may, but this is a serious matter," Monson emphasized. "No amount of success on the football field is worth breaking the law and contaminating your body. That one boy, Skoronski, had visible side effects."

"Yeah, why was his face so strange?"

"He had Acromegaly, which they tell me is a medical condition not uncommon for HGH users. There's overgrowth of facial bone and connective tissue, and that leads to changed appearance like a protruding jaw and eyebrow bones. You also get hair growth all over the body."

"So that's why Luke's looking so ugly," I remarked.

"That's the least of the problems," the detective said. "Acromegaly will shorten your life expectancy considerably."

I was wondering if the police had talked to Marla. I had to feel him out on that.

"Will the court need testimony from me or anybody else in this case?" I asked.

"It's possible," he replied, "but we have the confessions, so I doubt we'll need you."

I felt a little better as I hung up the phone.

On Friday morning, Frederick came rushing up to me at the start of school. "Did you hear about Coach Dawson?" he blurted out.

"No, what?"

"He's resigned. It was in the *Hillsboro Times* this morning, and it's on their website."

"What? You're kidding me?! Do you have the paper?"

Frederick reached into his backpack and pulled it out. "They think he knew about it, or should have known about it. I don't know if the school forced him out or he went on his own."

I quickly scanned the story. Coach Dawson made it sound like he knew nothing about HGH in his locker room.

"How was I supposed to know? They could have been going through natural growth spurts. Kids get bigger and stronger all the time," he argued in the article.

I looked up from the paper. "Do you think he knew?" I asked Frederick.

"I have to confess something," Frederick said, his eyes darting back and forth. "I told him about Palumbo and the infection. He chose to ignore it."

"Wow! Why do you think Dawson looked the other way? Was it all about winning?"

"Maybe. Or maybe he just didn't want to get involved. But the health of his players is his main responsibility. It's more important than anything — including winning."

I looked back down at the paper. "Is he gone immediately?"

"Uh-huh. It says so in the story."

Suddenly, I was beginning to feel let down. "We're getting a new coach? Spring practice is in another week!"

"Looks that way. I don't know who it's going to be."

I always had a good relationship with Coach Dawson. Now I was a victim of my own story.

"That stinks! Now I have to start from scratch with another coach," I complained.

"You and everybody else," Frederick said. "But maybe it's for the best, in your case. I'll sure be following you guys next year, even though I'm graduating."

Lunch time rolled around, and I was still the center of attention. People kept coming up to our table, asking me questions or commenting about the story, just like they had the past few days. Some were friendly, but others wanted to tell me off.

"You were just trying to bring down the football team," one guy charged.

"Why would I do that? I'm *on* the football team," I answered back.

"Yeah, well, you may be back on crutches after this. I'd watch out for blindside hits if I were you."

I just shook my head at the thought. The guy probably didn't realize, I'd already been blindsided. Still, I wondered if my teammates would take it out on me. I envisioned being gang-tackled whenever I touched the ball in practice.

Another kid — a senior on the newspaper, no less — called me out on my reporting credentials.

"You're just some punk who's trying to make a name for himself. You didn't know squat about reporting six months ago. All of a sudden you think you're Woodward? I don't even believe the story's true."

"Believe it. It's true," I shot back.

One kid, who I didn't know at all, just walked by and uttered a single word:

"Snitch."

Most of the guys on the team were keeping their distance, including Greg. I must have been some kind of pariah to them.

"Have you looked into the witness protection program?" Kevin joked. "Maybe they can hide you out in Montana."

I was thinking of something witty to say back when Max kicked me under the table. "Look who's coming," he whispered.

I looked up to see Greg walking our way. I didn't know whether to stay and talk to him or run. We hadn't spoken since the bathroom assault, and I was beginning to wonder if we'd ever speak again. I didn't know what to do, so I just stood up.

As he headed toward me, I looked straight at him. I could see daggers in his eyes. I braced myself in case he suddenly started charging. People parted like he was Moses walking through the Red Sea, allowing Greg a clear path.

I nervously racked my brain. What was I going to say? What *could* I say?

Closer and closer he got, until he stopped in front of me, his hulking presence less than two feet away.

"I just want to know one thing," Greg said, poking me in the chest. "Why did you write that story?"

"I'm s-o-r-r-y, Greg. I j-u-s-t thought it was the only way to help you," I stammered out.

"Help me?! By putting it in the paper?"

"I never used your name," I pointed out. "I wouldn't do that, because you're my friend."

"That's a pretty messed up way to treat a friend!" he yelled. "You ruined my life!"

"If I could have gotten you off it any other way, I would have. I tried, but you wouldn't listen."

"What do you mean you tried? You just ran off and wrote something in the paper!"

"No, I came to you a couple of times, remember? The last time you attacked me in the bathroom."

"You're lucky I didn't really hurt you!" I gulped at the thought.

"You don't need that crap! You're plenty good without it." Greg seemed to accept the compliment, but the veins in his neck were still bulging.

"You're okay now, right? You're not supposed to do jail time, are you?"

"I gotta get past probation and stay clean. But I will," he assured me.

"I know you will. And I'm still your friend," I said.

I was hoping Greg might say the same thing back, even though I knew there wasn't much chance of it. Instead he stormed off. "Spring practice starts next week. See you there!"

But that encounter with Greg wasn't the worst of it. When I checked my mail slot in the newsroom earlier in the day, I found an ominous note scribbled on a small piece of unlined paper:

Dear traitor, I'm gonna kill yu for backstabbing the team

I showed it to Gina. "That's kinda scary," she said. "I don't know if it's serious or not, but I'd turn it over to the police if I were you. You can't be too careful."

"I'm going to," I replied, more than a little shaken. I stashed the note in my pocket, trying to block it out of my mind. But I remembered the words Mr. McCloud said to me one September day:

"At the very least, journalists run the risk of making enemies when they honestly report stories."

⚊⚊⚊

That afternoon, the P.A. system interrupted science class again.

"Jason Jefferson, please report to the main office immediately."

What now? Wasn't I done with this?

I trudged down to the office wondering what I could be in trouble for. Did the police need more information? I worried that they would still grill me for the name of 'Deep Throat.'

Was I going to be handed court papers? Was I being sued?

Principal Healey met me as soon as I stepped into the office.

"Jason, there are some reporters outside who want to interview you."

He led me outside the front of the school, where the collection of assembled media made my eyes bug out. The News Channel 4 truck was parked directly in front of the building. Miles Cannon stood there with a microphone, alongside a cameraman. News 12 was there too, along with loads of other people holding tape recorders and notebooks.

I stepped outside and they swarmed around me like bees to honey. This was all for me?

Cannon jabbed a microphone in my face. "Jason Jefferson, how does it feel to break the blockbuster story about drug use on the Hillsboro High football team?"

"Uh ... I don't know. I have mixed feelings."

Miles didn't seem to listen to my answer. "You must be very proud of yourself. For a high school kid to get this story before the seasoned pros in the media ..."

I considered that remark. It's true, I did beat the great Miles Cannon to a story, the same Miles Cannon who acted like God's gift to journalism when he visited our classroom.

"Thank you Miles. I just pursued this story like it was Watergate. I ran into some obstacles, but I never gave up."

"Who was your main source?" Miles asked. "Where did you get your information?"

"I got my information from good old-fashioned report-ing, and I'm not going to reveal my main source."

Miles looked at me peculiarly. "But the drug offenders have already been taken into custody?"

"I know, but I protect my sources. Loyalty is more important to me than grabbing a sound bite on TV."

Miles looked put off. "Not even on News Channel 4 and our millions of viewers in the Chicago area?"

"Not even on News Channel 4. I'm sorry."

Miles jerked his microphone away and backed off, but another mike shot in to fill the void. "Bill Dennis from Channel 12, Jason. We heard a rumor that human growth hormone was only part of it. Is it true that Coach Dawson supplied anabolic steroids to the entire team?"

"That's totally false. I don't know where you got that," I answered. "Have you spoken to the police? I think they'll refute that too."

"You're on the football team too, and I've heard you're friends with one of the players arrested. Did that make it extra hard to write this story for your school paper?" Dennis asked.

"It sure did. Like I said before, I had mixed emotions. But I knew toward the end that I was doing the right thing."

"That has to give you great satisfaction. But do you still have any regrets?"

"Not in reporting the story. Of course, I regret that the players were using HGH in the first place."

I thought for a few seconds before adding something else. "And I regret that I falsely believed another player who was completely innocent was involved. I'd like to make a public apology to Pete Cruz."

"The star linebacker?"

"Yes. I never accused him to his face, but I did suspect him throughout my investigation. I guess it goes to show reporters sometimes make mistakes ... even *Hillsboro Herald* reporters."

The reporters all laughed at my remark.

I answered a few more questions from the TV and radio reporters before the microphones began to retreat. Then another wave of reporters — the newspaper and web guys — circled me for more. One guy hit me with a question I wasn't ready for.

"Jason, do you think Hillsboro should be stripped of its state title? After all, indications are the players were using performance-enhancing drugs during the season. They cheated."

The reporter made a good point. But I wasn't about to throw more gas on the fire.

"I don't think so," I replied. "The whole team worked really hard, and most of them weren't even involved. I think it would be unfair to those players if someone took the title away."

"But that happens all the time in sports — everyone on the team gets penalized for the inappropriate actions of a few," he pointed out.

"You're right," I said, squirming in my sneakers. "But that's not for me to decide."

"What about Coach Dawson's resignation? Do you think he should have resigned?"

I wish I could have said, "You should direct that question to my attorney," but I had no one to hand off the tough questions to. I felt a little tinge of sadness for Dawson. He was always nice to me.

"I don't know, I think that decision was up to Coach Dawson, or whoever makes those decisions."

Eventually, the car doors slammed shut and the media began to drive away to chase the next "hot" story. But just as everyone else pulled away, Miles Cannon jumped forward one last time.

"I need an exclusive," I heard him say to his cameraman. Then he shoved his microphone back in my face.

"Jason, could you give us the name of the boy who sold the HGH, the main culprit in the scandal?"

I smiled back, but held my ground. "No I can't, Miles. I think we should protect his rights."

"What about the public's right to know? This criminal tried to ruin the lives of others!"

"He's not a criminal! He's just a kid who made a big mistake," I fired back. "And he's under 18. You should know not to reveal his name."

Cannon stormed off, muttering something to the cameraman. He didn't even thank me for the interview like the others did.

I watched with amusement as the Great Miles Cannon drove away.

On Monday morning, I was summoned again from class. Only this time, Mrs. Polansky came and personally escorted me to the principal's office. "What's this about?" I asked her, but she wouldn't say. I grudgingly started to follow her, and she hurried me along.

When we got to the office, Principal Healey handed me the phone. "Someone wants to talk to you."

I pulled the phone to my ear. "Hello?"

"Hello Jason, this is Bob Woodward."

I smirked and looked over at Healey. It had to be Max or Kevin playing a joke. But if it was, Healey sure was fooled. His face looked normal.

"I'm in the area, and I read about your story," the voice said. "You did a remarkable reporting job."

My jaw dropped and I looked over at Healey again. He just nodded. I began to believe it really was Bob Woodward.

"H-o-w-w did you he-a-r-r about it?" I stuttered.

"It made the Chicago Tribune," the caller said. "I'm here on business and I saw it in Sunday's paper. I'm originally from this area, you know. I grew up in Wheaton."

"That's right! I remember you said that in 'All the President's Men.'"

"Oh, so you read my book?"

"And I saw the movie," I pointed out. "They were both awesome!"

"Nice of you to say that. I was flattered to have Robert Redford play me in the movie. I never looked that good."

I couldn't believe *the* Bob Woodward, the driving force behind the Watergate investigation, the man who brought down a president who committed illegal acts, was on the phone with me.

"I really think you showed remarkable investigative reporting instincts for a young man your age. It's not often a high school student breaks a story like that. I just called the school to congratulate you."

I straightened up, proud as a peacock.

"It's a shame," Woodward continued. "Real enterprise reporting is hard to find these days. Too often investigative reporting is the first to go when the media make budget cuts. And unfortunately, without investigative reporters, corruption runs rampant. You see it in Washington, but there are scandals everywhere. We need people like you to root them out."

"Thanks." The whole conversation, with Bob Woodward complimenting me, seemed surreal.

Finally, I forced something out. "It was hard for me, Mr. Woodward. One of my friends was involved. At times, I didn't know whether the story was worth it."

"Of course it was, Jason. You broke an important story and you may have saved your friend's life."

"That's what I'm hoping ... uh, the second part."

"Journalists *can* make a difference," Woodward stressed.

"You really did. After your Watergate reporting and the Vietnam War, people don't look at government the same. People really question things now."

"As well they should," Woodward remarked. "That's our right in a democracy."

There was a moment of silence on the line as I soaked in what he said.

"Look, I'm at O'Hare. I've got to catch a flight back to Washington," Woodward said. "But let me give you my email address. Feel free to contact me if you have any questions about reporting. You have a bright future in journalism, young man."

I grabbed a pen off Healey's desk and jotted down the email address. I couldn't wait to tell Mr. McCloud about the call.

CHAPTER 27

Several days after turning over the anonymous death threat note to Detective Monson, I gave him a call. I was still concerned about my safety, to say the least, always looking over my shoulder.

"We've evaluated it, and we don't believe it's a credible threat," Monson said. "Go on living your life, Jason. We don't know who sent it, but we think it was just some hothead who never intended to act on it, or it was just a hoax."

I breathed a deep sigh of relief.

I managed to make it through spring practice in one piece. Maybe it was good that we didn't wear pads, so there was no hitting.

Rumors flew around that we were going to be stripped of our state championship. I was nervous as hell, because I knew a lot of people would blame me. But it never happened. I guess the Illinois High School Association didn't have any specific rules in place about human growth hormone. Maybe they didn't think it could reach into the high schools until the Hillsboro scandal. But it did.

As for the offenders, Greg, Mike and Luke were under-classmen, but they got clean and remained on the team. It was probably a good thing we didn't have a head coach in place; there was no one to throw them off.

Or it could have been that Hillsboro High just wanted to put the incident behind. All the media publicity left a scar that no one wanted to talk about. It was time to move on.

When we did get a new head coach in July, he barely made reference to the past, except to talk about the school's great winning tradition. Coach Montelli was confident we were going to continue that tradition.

One day I asked one of the assistant coaches whatever happened to Coach Dawson.

"I hear he's coaching in Indiana," Coach Baker said. "I think he's in Gary."

"That's good," I replied. I felt kind of bad for Dawson. He was a casualty in the whole mess because he didn't get involved. But he should have. I wondered if he was watching his players more closely in his new job.

The HGH controversy eventually died down. Summer, with its respite from school, seemed to heal a lot of wounds. By the time we returned in the fall, I felt accepted on the team. Guys were mostly concerned about keeping our win-ning streak alive. I had most of my speed back — although I couldn't say the knee was as strong as it was before the injury.

And I couldn't say my relationship with Greg was ful-ly mended, either. Like the knee, it was workable, but not perfect. We didn't speak again until August, and even then the conversations lacked the same enthusiasm on his part.

When Greg spoke to me it was mostly from his role as tri-captain, like it was his responsibility. There wasn't any warmth.

I know he was fretting over his scholarship offer from Notre Dame. He was afraid they'd rescind it. When word got out that he had taken HGH, some colleges backed off.

"You may have screwed me royally," he said to me one day.

That made me question myself again. Did I do the right thing?

Fortunately, winning cures a lot of ills. As the new season began, we ran our winning streak to 17 games, and Greg was more of a force than ever. He was relentless, almost like he was made of metal and the ballcarrier was a magnet. The Barbarian was back with a vengeance.

After one home game, I noticed Greg talking to a man outside the locker room. The man wore a dark blue hat with the gold letters "ND" embroidered on the front.

From that day on, Greg was all smiles. He seemed more relaxed than ever.

"Was that a Notre Dame recruiter you were talking to?" I asked.

"Sure was! They still want to give me a full ride!"

"Wow! To South Bend? You deserve it, man. I'm happy for you! I know that's where you really want to go."

"Always has been," Greg acknowledged. "I was just worried they'd back off too. You know ... because of the mistake I made."

BOB MOSELEY

"I guess Notre Dame believes in second chances," I said. Greg flashed me an easy smile, the first one I'd received from him in a long time.

We stretched our winning streak to 18 games by knocking off Plano 27-21 a week later. There had to be 15,000 fans there. It was insane — the most memorable sporting event I ever played in. That's because I came off the bench to score the winning touchdown on a 10-yard sweep.

Greg was the first one to congratulate me. He raced onto the field and practically knocked me over, before hoisting me above his shoulders into the warm Texas night.

I'll never forget that game — or Greg's gesture. I felt like we'd finally turned the page.

CHAPTER 28: 10 YEARS LATER

G reg Maxwell, with bleached blond hair, strode into the Hillsboro High School auditorium—all 6-foot-3, 240 pounds of him. The crowd bubbled in anticipation. Some students even jumped out of their seats to get autographs, only to be told by their teachers to sit back down.

The principal led him to the front, where a microphone lay on a podium on the stage. She tapped it and pulled it to her face. "Testing one-two-three, testing one-two-three."

As the principal adjusted the volume, I got up from my seat in the front row and tapped Greg on the shoulder. His face lit up like a bonfire.

"Jason! Man, how are ya?" he exclaimed, giving me a hug. He squeezed with the same caring grasp he had that day in high school when I wrecked my knee and he carried me off the football field. "Great to see you! Do you still live in town?"

Before I could answer, the principal motioned Greg to the stage, looking confident that the mike was adjusted properly.

"Stick around, man. Let's catch up after this," Greg said, patting me on the shoulder before walking up the side steps to the stage. The applause got louder with each stair he scaled.

"Let's quiet down," the principal announced, holding the mike in one hand and raising her other arm up high. A few teachers, only one of whom I recognized from my high school days, lined the walls at the front of the auditorium and peered out over the students.

"Today we are pleased to have a Hillsboro High School alumnus come back to speak to us, one who has gone on to accomplish great things in the world of sports. Greg Maxwell was an All-American at the University of Notre Dame who became a first-round NFL draft pick. He's now an All-Pro linebacker with the San Diego Chargers and a role model for all of us who dream about reaching our goals. I'm so happy he could join us today while his team is in town to play our Bears. Just don't beat us, Greg."

The students laughed and cheered her request. Chants of "Let's Go Bears!" broke out in the auditorium.

She raised her hand again to quiet the crowd. "Without further ado, I give you Greg Maxwell."

"Thank-you Principal Hargraves," Greg acknowledged, when the applause finally subsided. "When I look out at you students here today I see myself, because I was once just like you, facing the challenges and temptations that teens encounter growing up. It's not easy. Sometimes we can get off-track as we try to reach our goals.

"I want to talk to you today about the choices we make in life. When you're growing up, sometimes you make the wrong choice. We all make mistakes. I know I did. Sometimes you want something so bad, the only way you think you can achieve it is to take shortcuts. But that's not the answer.

"I was fortunate. I had some people around me who set me straight. One of them is now my wife, and one of them is sitting here today," he said, looking down at me in the front row. "I love them for it. Oh, at first I felt betrayed. I couldn't accept anyone butting into my life. But as time went on I realized that they were acting in my best interest. I thank God for friends like that. I hope you're surrounded by people like that too.

"Sometimes we make bad choices in life. Sometimes we need friends and family to set us straight."

I sat there amazed. After all these years, Greg still regretted his teenage reliance on human growth hormone. And he never forgot my effort to get him off it.

For the next 10 minutes, Greg spoke to the students about what it takes to reach your goals. Then he answered questions for another 15 minutes. When the assembly ended, he hurried over to me.

"That was a great speech," I said. "You had the kids spellbound."

"I meant every word of it," he replied. "You saved my life." He gave me another hug.

"It's great to see you. I hear you're working for News Channel 4 in Chicago. Is that right?"

"Yeah, I got a job right out of Northwestern. I'm now the station's investigative reporter. It's great."

"Cool! Hey, I can't believe you even got into Northwestern in the first place," he said, stepping back like he was awestruck.

"I know," I said with a chuckle. "The letter of recommendation from Bob Woodward sure helped. Gina Giantoli and I both made it into the Medill school of journalism."

"Awesome! Good school," Greg remarked.

"How's Marla?" I asked.

"She's pregnant," Greg said, flashing a wide smile. "She's due in about three months, right after the season. The doctor says it's a boy."

"Congratulations! He's gonna be a bruiser like his dad."

"Yeah, Marla already feels him kicking in there."

"How do you like living in San Diego?"

"We love it! We've got a place right on the beach in Oceanside."

"I can tell. You look like a surfer with the blond hair."

"I do surf. Man, it's gorgeous out there. You gotta come out and visit us sometime."

I imagined Marla in a bathing suit. Then I remembered she was pregnant.

"Hey, remember the Plano game? You helped us win it."

"How could I forget? It was my first varsity touchdown. I don't know if I ever got all my speed back, but I became a starter the next year, you know. I rushed for 1,000 yards and made all-conference as a senior."

"Good for you! I remember we only lost one game my last year, in the playoffs to Crystal Lake, or we would have had back-to-back unbeaten seasons."

"Rob Kelley's fumble," I recalled. "That cost us the game."

"Please, don't remind me. I was bummed out for a week. But, you know, looking back, I was just lucky to be playing. I could have gotten kicked off the team."

"Greg, I would have felt as bad as you if that happened."

"I know," he said softly, putting his hand on my shoulder. "It took me a while to get over things, but everything worked out for the best. I was crazy back then. I don't know where I'd be today if I'd stayed on that stuff."

"Hey Greg, have you ever run into Cruz after high school?"

"We played Oklahoma State in a bowl game one year, but Pete was injured and didn't play. I never had a problem with Pete. I think he just resented that I was getting more attention than him. I understand that."

Greg paused for a moment. "Whatever happened to the little guy who was student-trainer my junior year? What was his name?"

"Frederick."

"Yeah, Frederick. That dude took his job seriously. Remember the time he tore across the field to treat Kelley's knee and tripped over the water bucket? Then he got up and the bucket was caught on his foot. He couldn't get it off."

"I was a sophomore then, but I was at that game. It was hilarious!" I recalled. "I got a call from Frederick about a year ago. He's the assistant trainer at the University of Illinois."

"Nice. That suits him perfectly," Greg said. The auditorium was empty now. We began to walk up the incline to the back and the exit.

"I know about one other person you might be interested in — Sara," I teased.

Greg stopped walking. "No! What's up with her?"

"She's engaged. I saw it in the paper. She met the guy in college at Southern Illinois."

Greg broke into a broad smile. "I'm happy for her. Sara's a great girl."

We continued toward the exit. There was a moment of silence before Greg made me an offer I couldn't refuse.

"Why don't you come to the game Sunday? I'll leave you a pair of tickets at the will-call window. You have anyone special you'd like to take?"

"Yeah, I'm dating someone from the station. We've been going together for about two years now."

"All right! Stop by the locker room afterward. I'd love to meet her."

"We'll be there!"

"The only thing is, I can't let you inside the locker room. If the guys see a famous investigative reporter, they'll freak," Greg said with a laugh.

"That's cool," I said, smiling back.

Exiting the auditorium and slowly walking toward the front doors of the school, we passed the trophy case, stuffed with awards and memories from glory days past.

"Look at that," Greg said, pointing at a football that formed the centerpiece of the display. "Undefeated State Champions. 14-0. Ranked No. 1 in Illinois. Those were great days, Jason."

"Most of them," I remarked.

"Most of them," Greg agreed.

We said goodbye and went our separate ways. Greg had to get back for a late afternoon practice and I had to edit tape with my producer. As usual, I was working on something big.

But on my way back to Chicago, I drove by the corner of Brighton and Travers for a look at the field where we played tackle football games in our youth. The field looked the same — maybe a little smaller than I remembered — except for one striking change: A large sign posted said the lot was under development.

Just like our lives.

When I arrived at the newsroom, Miles Cannon was wrapping up the 6 p.m. broadcast. The cameras zoomed in on him as he sat behind the anchor's desk, looking sincere.

"Be sure to tune in tomorrow. You won't want to miss Jason Jefferson's investigative report from Springfield: 'Corruption at the Capitol.' "

CPSIA information can be obtained at www.ICGtesting.com
Printed in the USA
LVOW040730181012

303231LV00001B/243/P